CW00539682

Edited by the incomparable
Katarina Yerger.

katraeyerger@gmail.com
https://www.clippings.me/katarinayerger

You did a great job, Thank you!

"Abstain from every form of evil."
1 Thessalonians 5:22

DARK DESCENDANTS

STACEY L. PIERSON

ANUCI PRESS

First paperback edition May 2024

Anuci Press edition May 2024
www.anuci-press.com

Book cover design by Adrian Medina
fabledbeastdesign@gmail.com
fabledbeastdesign.wordpress.com

ISBN 979-8-9896198-4-9 (paperback)

CHAPTER 1
FUCKING FINKLE

EVEN IF YOU wake up in the light, the dark is always watching.

Being dubbed "the town drunk" didn't bother Jacob Finkle, the second Finkle. He embraced it, scribbling his name on his thin and tattered jean jacket, which smelled of cigarette smoke. Residents turned up their noses at the sour and unwashed stench emanating from him and his jacket while walking down the sidewalk. Nonetheless, he held his head high, as if running for political office, as he drank vodka shots at Sadie's Bar.

It has always amazed bar owner Robert Walser and Finkle's childhood friend, how he could drink that much every single day and function in the morning. Either way, Robert is glad to take his money. Robert glances over to the clock sitting on the wall as he dries a glass with a red dingy rag.

"Closing time."

As he looks around, he notices Finkle with his head down. With his nose in the glass, he appears to be smelling the last sip, and Robert gazes, annoyed since it's been a long day. Robert uses a loud and hard knock on the counter to get Finkle's attention, which it does. Finkle flings one of his arms over his head like a cowboy on a bull ride, then "ahhhhs" before looking at Robert through the bottom of the shot glass like his version of rose-colored glasses. Robert stares at him, knowing that Finkle will never remember the times Robert has taken him home, stopped him from stealing other customers' drinks from their hands and tables, or let him sleep it off in the backroom.

"It's time for you to go home, Jacob," Robert urges in a strict voice like a father telling his son to finish his homework.

Finkle leans back and scoffs as he points his finger and stares at Robert. Wasted, Finkle chuckles, almost falling off the chair. He catches himself and squeaks his hand against the bar's edge. The shot glass rolls across the counter.

"I despise that name. My father's name was Jacob, and he made my life a living hell. That bastard," Finkle slurs as he reclines on the stool. "I'm not at all like him. And none of you can say that I am. Finkle. My name is Finkle."

"Whatever you say, Jacob."

"It's been a long day, and I can't deal with you all night. So…" Robert motions his head toward the front door.

"You want me to go out there? Let me tell you something…there's a lot of darkness out there," Finkle tells him as he points outside.

"No shit. It's nighttime."

Waiting for something more from Robert, frustrated Finkle gets up and heads for the front door. He stops midway.

"You have no idea what's out there. All you know is this," Finkle looks around the bar, "life."

Robert turns his back as he continues to clean the mess Finkle made. His breath fogs up the glass as he stares into the oncoming darkness. The sun dips behind the treetops as Finkle peers out the door's window. He then focuses on the golden cursive letters that spell "Sadie's Place." Finkle lowers his head, turns slowly, and traces the edge of the letter E.

"Do you miss her?" Finkle asks.

Startled, Robert breaks a glass in his hand. His breathing becomes labored, and he never looks Finkle's way as his other hand forms a fist. A wave of cold anger furrows his brows as he tries to keep calm and speak to Finkle.

"Never ask me that again. You don't have the right. No one does."

"I know, but listen to me," Finkle responds.

Finkle trips over his feet as he steps forward and lands on a table with small brown baskets, spilling empty peanut shells all over the floor. That's more work for Robert, who watches Finkle look down and begin to pick up the baskets.

"You haven't changed a bit since we were kids. You're still worthless but now, you're crazy. Just like your momma was."

Finkle drops the baskets and mumbles, "I would rather be crazy than blind."

Finkle is on his feet. He crushes the baskets beneath his boots, grabs a few napkin dispensers, and tosses them across the bar, where they collide with the wall, knocking off a dart board. He kicks stools, particularly the one he was sitting in, and knocks several tables over on their sides. He kicks the front door open with his back leg while giving Robert the bird and mouthing the words "fuck you."

But he forgets one thing and never notices it until it's too late.

To say Louisiana's weather is confusing is an understatement. Residents must adapt, especially if they live near the water, as Finkle does. It's not rare like in other parts of the world, but Mother Nature likes to play games during the summer. Tonight is one of those games. Full of energy, Finkle re-enacts his kicks and tosses while bobbing back and forth like Rocky. He looks at his empty hands and stops. He snaps his head behind him as he realizes he left his lantern at Sadie's Bar. He turns back to retrieve it. He will grovel if he must. It wouldn't be the first time. Having no shame, he turns around and pauses. The ground behind him is covered like a blanket of darkness. A chilly wind rush through and around Finkle. He decides to press on and get home as fast as possible. He hurriedly across the street and into the buzzing streetlight, pulling his jacket tighter around him and burying his face in his hands.

It's getting later and later. No one is outside. Finkle stays on guard as he knows most of the time, people have their porch lights turned on, if not their interior lights and the only sound is the rustle of leaves chasing each other down the middle of the street. As he walks faster, Finkle passes the leaves and realizes he can't hear them move.

With a slight weave, Finkle adjusts many times while walking. Almost bumping into an old truck with rust breaking through the silver paint, stepping down and back up onto the curb. In the bushes ahead, they move, and he stops. It stops. He takes another step, and the shaking starts back up. With one foot hovering above the ground, the bush shakes, and a cat meows, leaping out.

He stumbles backward and lands in the middle of the street where the streetlights look like they are holding hands. With his hands on his knees, he tries to catch his breath. Laughing in between, he watches the cat run around the corner. Standing, he exhales to the sky with his hands on his hips, walking around and looking around, relieved.

"It's just a cat. Oh my god, thank you. It's just a cat."

Then something catches his eye, and he holds his breath, stopping.

A lady in her sixties, wearing a bright pink moo-moo and matching furry slippers, stands at her sink, washing dishes.

She wears an oatmeal and egg facemask and rollers made of small tomato paste cans clinched tightly under a silky hairnet. She bobs her head as she rinses plates. As the water runs, she sings off-key to a song on the radio to her left, sitting on a shelf with a cigarette half-gone in the black ashtray. When she hears something mixing with the music, wondering what is happening, she runs her hands through the damp hand towel resting on the sink's edges and lowers the music. She narrows her eyes as a figure comes into view.

She looks out the window and sees Finkle running, yelling at the top of his lungs. She shakes her head and takes a drag on a cigarette as she follows him with her eyes. Ashes fall off the edge and into the sink's soap. Finkle trips. He hits the ground hard as he belly-flops on the road, and his lower body rises into the air. The woman bursts out laughing and spits her cigarette into the sink. He scrambles to his feet, and he continues. As she lights another cigarette, she shakes her head.

"Fucking Finkle," she says as she turns the music back up.

As perspiration accumulates on Finkle's forehead and slides down his face, he grips his side. The pain is stabbing. He was never an athlete. Even when bullies chased him in high school, he was always caught. It's the same thing this time. If he stops, he will be caught again. He starts to slow down, heavy-footed and tired. Out of breath, he stops. He looks over his shoulder. The first streetlight he had stood under begins to flicker and dim.

The streetlight goes out. Finkle stands. He squints his eyes and stares. He doesn't see anything. Another streetlight goes out. He takes a step back. A third streetlight blows out. A pungent, foul odor of rotten meat creeps into his nostrils. Finkle hunches over and retches. He covers his mouth as the

5

contents of his stomach swirl and itch. But he is powerless to stop it. A delicious pale and yellow tint of beer spurted out and landed in an opaque color, burning a portion of the pavement in front of him.

He wipes the vomit strings that dangle from his chin. He looks down to see his boot tips bent in, and he steps back to see his boot rubber melting. As he steps back, a tickle runs up his spine and intertwines in his hairline.

The last lightbulb crunches beneath something large and powerful. Finkle's heartbeat sharpens, and the left side of his face begins to scoop down. Another step crushes the second lightbulb's shard. Finkle's hands become numb. He tries to keep them from crawling up his arms, but they have already reached his forearms. He loses coordination and buckles at the knees. Drool dribbles from the side of his mouth as he stares into the patch of growing darkness that he desperately wants to run from. But he can't. Then an endless low-level childish giggle suckles the air from the street, and slivers of the third lightbulb bounce from the darkness.

He can't move. He can't speak. He can't think. All he can do is watch and wait. He didn't have to wait long. Finkle comes face-to-face with darkness. A deep, hot exhale blows his hair in a wild gust, so strange that his skin chills and blushes an icy blue, causing him to piss himself as gummy saliva drop from the featureless darkness.

A roar fills the air.

CHAPTER 2
YOU'RE NOT GETTING A WARM WELCOME HOME

THIRTEEN MONTHS LATER

ON THE MAINLAND'S SHORE, gray seagulls squawk and caw. They sometimes react to the boats in the harbor as if they're playing a copycat game, and their ha-ha-can ha's and mock them. They dive in and out of the water, running back to shore as the waves swell. As the waves recede into the lake and reveal footprints, a pair of teal sneakers leave an imprint in the grittier sand.

A jogger's calves flex and tense with each step, and her shorts fit snugly around her slim thighs. But she never stops; as soon as the water reaches the tips of her sneakers, she runs through it to maintain her pace. She runs steadily, her burnt chocolate-colored ponytail bobbling side to side and grazing the white cords of her earpieces. Her earpieces connect to her iPhone, which is strapped to her upper arm around her long-sleeve gray shirt that hugs her chest and stomach. She keeps her gaze fixed on the sand. Her feet step in front of each other as if she were walking an imaginary tightrope. Boats dumping empty and filled cages for catching shrimp, lobster, and especially crawfish fill the water in the distance, speaking and making dirty jokes in Creole French.

"Qu'est-ce que la femme a dit au prêtre? Je veux faire une

confession, je connais un endroit. J'y étais hier soir. (What did the woman say to the priest? Wanna make a confession, I know a place. I was there last night.)"

While listening to music, her mouth blows out a long breath as men on a small boat near the dock can be heard in the background blowing high-pitched whistles. They summon her, but she never responds, keeping the focus on her end goal, which is the broken-down shack that sells bait to the fisherman. A seagull dives inches from her head and startles her, and she stumbles backward. She falls on her butt. For a moment, her hands vanish in the sand. Men on the boat laugh and talk to each as they look at her.

As she pulls the sand out and wipes her hands together, she notices it slipping into places that make her uncomfortable. Not the best feeling in the world, especially when people watch. As the sand falls, she flips them off. But they never see it because another boat floats in front of them.

Two men rush across the deck, carrying shrimp and crawfish cages up the boat's side and over the edge. She watches as they nearly lose one. They catch it, but the latch opens, allowing crawfish to fall onto the boat's deck. They laugh, shake their heads, and then high-five each other. She narrows her eyes and recognizes one of the men. It's Finkle. He yells and waves his hand at Isaiah Dodson, his boat-mate, employee, and friend. He stomps his leg on deck to get his attention.

Finkle, feeling like he's being watched, spots the jogger, and they stare at each other. They never make any motions, not even a smile, and then Finkle turns away as she stands. As he and the boat make their way to the middle of the lake, towards the other side. She dusts off the sand she fell into on the beach and pretends she never saw him. A phone rang, causing her to jump. She responds by touching her earpiece.

"Hello?"

She takes a deep breath and listens. Despite her best efforts not to, she glances at Finkle as his boat fades away.

"I'm on my way. Tell Ollie to meet me at the dock in thirty minutes. I'll need him."

She looks at the water one last time before hanging up the phone. The line of trees on the island across from her appears to be waving to her. She takes a deep breath and turns to run backward, following the steps she had just made in the sand.

———

The small boat's motor chugs along, sputtering but efficient enough, as the boat crashes and bounces off the choppy, mirror-like dark water of the bayou. The mainlanders call it The Mouth.

Semicircular, The Mouth is a collection of islands, many of which are bushy, some of which are mossy, and others that are no more than an arm's reach away from their nearest neighbor. Alligators regularly swim to the smaller ones to relax or to eat the fish, turtles, and unsuspecting birds that land nearby or on them. There are a few houses built on private islands, airboats as vehicles, docks with humps in the wood, and otters and river rats sunbathing before they become dinner. Other islands have wooden houseboats with parts rotting in the shallow end of the water. Murky trees sit motionless, tangled in moss, and alone. A small boat approaches the shore of an island.

Sunlight breaks through the sleepy white mist hanging on the bayou as they head toward a large island surrounded by rocks and pine trees. Pine Island. Home to a unique group of people known as the Islanders for over two hundred years, its beauty—flowers decorating the ground and the small beach-like setting—is breathless and calls to onlookers as bright green tree tops sway and swing in the breeze. However, mainlanders never go there unless they have too. Campfire and bedtime stories warn them of the dangers of cannibalistic living. Mainlanders and Islanders never interact or converse, even in passing. When it comes to something as simple as saying, "to each their own," to the Islanders, it means that mainlanders are not welcome.

With a splash, a leather police boot is consumed by the water. It soaks the black laces and the lower part of tan khaki pants and stains them with wild droplets, darkening sections of the pants. A brass belt buckle tightly wraps around the tan, tucked-in, button-down shirt. The sun shines down and catches the glare from a star. A sheriff's star which reads. "Finkle" in big, black, bold letters on a gold plate on the other side of the star.

Grabbing the corner of the boat, Therese 'Tre' Finkle pulls it closer to the dock. Using rope, she secures the dock edge. She slaps her hands on her pants and looks toward the driver in rubber overalls, a self-made tank top, and an old cap. He turns his head away and spits into the water. Narrowing her almond-shaped eyes, she sighs as the wind blows her dark hair, pinning wild pieces to her lips. Tre is average height, slender in stature, and carries herself with self-confidence no one can rock, not even a slight of-the-eye look. She scoffs.

Deputy Ollie Boden, a constant notetaker with black-rimmed glasses hanging on his nose and curly hair. Ollie always tries to impress Tre with the knowledge he googles and reads, even if the book is over ten years old. He struggles to get up and out the boat but eventually succeeds. Tre and Ollie begin walking down the dock. Green around the gills and silently burping under his breath, Ollie swallows hard.

"Let me guess. This is the first time you have ever been on the island."

"Is it that obvious?"

Tre chuckles as she pats him on the back.

"Nah, you just look like a fish out of water. If you wanna

puke hang your head over the side. I promise no one will judge you. Much."

"I'll remember that."

Uneven due to the water, the dock's planks swell, the posts tremble, and the thud sounds from the soles of their rubber boots echo and call for attention. Ollie begins to pull out a small black notebook and click the tip of his pen, but Tre pushes it downward.

"Write down everything you hear, no matter what it is. I seriously doubt Jamieson will tell us everything."

"Who's he?"

"An old friend of mine."

Tre sighs as she bears down her stare at a man waiting for them at the end of the dock with his hands on his hips. His stance resembles of those old Western shows where the good and bad guys stand looking at each other in a duel to the death. Marshall Jamieson Spence is as lanky as a hungry scarecrow, with a godlike stance; he might as well hold a staff in one hand and keep the other handy to grab his handcuffs. The large brim of his hat casts a shadow on his face, making him look unshaven and angry. Ollie quickly notices that Marshall Spence has no weapons, or anything like them.

"Yeah, he doesn't look happy to see us," Ollie says with warning and interest.

"It's not us."

Tre places her hand on her wide black garrison duty-issued belt. One side is suited with her 9mm Glock, and on the other side, she has necessities like mace and a flashlight, and in the back is a taser. That's not counting the small knife that slipped next to the handcuffs inside its holster. Tre takes a deep breath as they step off the dock and stop a few feet away from Marshall Spence.

"Morning Jamieson."

"It's Marshall Spence to you, Tre."

Ollie feels the power pull happening between them along

with the tempered tension that's rising quicker than the flutters inside his stomach.

"It's Sheriff Finkle to you, Marshall Spence."

The rumor of Tre and Jamieson's past as teenagers spread among the Islanders as if they were emotionally and sexually involved. People expected their wedding to be the highlight of the year, and their anniversary to be the party of the month and for many months after. But it never came to pass. He proposed, but Tre declined. It quickly turned sour. Despite the years apart, the bitter taste remains on the tip of his tongue.

"How about you get back in your shitty little boat and go back down the mouth where you came from? There's nothing here I can't handle."

"Well, that changes everything. Deputy Boden, make sure you have that down exactly as Marshall Spence has suggested."

Tre leans into Ollie as he writes, and says, "No. It's not… wait let me check." She turns to Marshall Spence. "Was that piece of shit or shitty? I just want to make sure I have it right for my report. The report I have to make to my boss."

Marshall Spence straightens his back and knows he has no choice but to let Tre on his island, as he likes to call it. Tre rolls her eyes.

"Look, you're not the one paying me, so how about you step back and let Deputy Boden, and I determine if everything is peachy clean? Then we'll leave."

Marshall Spence puffs out his cheeks and sucks his tongue against his upper teeth. He gives Tre a disgruntled and cold glare as he adjusts his pants, hiking them up slightly to reveal his thin, unnoticeable pecker, which he believes is enormous.

"I thought you said he was an old friend of yours."

"Did I? Why don't you start over there with that group staring us down? I think you'll have some luck."

"Sure thing," Ollie says, swiftly walking off.

Marshall Spence is talking to Islanders out of the corner of

Tre's eyes, and the looks they give her are rough and crude. She doesn't have to be aware that her presence has sparked controversy on the island. She can already feel the hatred from all sides where she stands, especially from the small group that has gathered, and more are gathering at the end of a long wooden log-style porch, shooting daggers.

The burnt-out sign reads "Quills," the local general and only store that sells household staples. Eggs, milk, orange juice, soda, candy, and magazines. But for Islanders, household staples mean potted meat more than likely out of date, bottles of water instead of soda because it's bad for the teeth, the only magazine would be an old TV guide from the seventies with Goldie Hawn as the pin-up girl (especially the picture from Laugh-In) and butter churners. It makes for a great movie night. Islanders live off the land by the bundles of flowers you can buy for decorating or snacking on with friends.

Tre looks at each of the Islanders at Quills, seething with anger as they scowl, glancing at each other and asking silent questions themselves, such as *when she is going to leave. How can she possibly return? Will anyone miss her if she goes missing?* They keep smiling because they know the answer is no. No one would miss her because they haven't.

Across the road, Tre notices a flyer nailed to a post with a frayed corner. After walking toward it, she stops. She examines a photograph of Colby Morel, a sixteen-year-old boy with bright eyes and a sweet smile. She looks around perplexed. The flyer that arrived at her office via wire is completely different. She quickly removes it. They're at least two years apart in age. She received a photograph that is older and more mature, with a more defined cleft chin. The one in her hand has smoother skin and a smaller cleft in the chin. She is aware that something is wrong. She notices several of the Islanders who have dispersed after leaving Quills' porch.

13

One man leans against another man while chewing on a piece of pine straw. A woman halfway lays on the hood of an old truck, drums her fingers slowly, and tries to intimate Tre as she passes, and Tre gives her a big, bright smile. Three young girls straddle their bikes, whispering to one another as their parents rush up to protect them from Tre, who waves her fingers at them. Lastly, a group of Islanders blocks Colby's parents from her like a strong protest line, but they are not fighting for something right or equal. Still, they keep her from them. So, Tre bends down a little and peers through the crack of two men to see Colby's mother weeping and falling apart in her husband's arms.

Mr. Morel darts his eyes at Tre as he pulls his wife closer and whispers something in her ear, never breaking his stare at Tre. His wife turns and looks at her. Tre leans up. The two men stare down at her.

"See, here's the problem. The longer you refuse to let me do my job, the longer I have to stay on the island. And let's be honest, I want to leave just as much as you do."

In the background, she hears a knock, and they step aside. She slips through them and smiles. "Thank you."

Tre approaches the Morels, clutching Colby's flyer. But she pauses before speaking. It's difficult to speak to someone who has their back turned and is ignoring her. Tre smirks as she realizes what this means. She reaches for her radio, which is positioned on her shoulder.

"Deputy Boden?"

"Yeah, Sheriff?" Boden answers with a click of the radio.

"If you're not too busy, mind coming over to Quills? "

"Headed over right now."

Patient, Tre places her hand behind her back and rocks on her heels. She waves to an elderly woman in a flowery white and yellow dress, holding a large bag hung on her silver walker with tennis balls on the front legs, who is staring at her. She runs her thumb over the flyer's single pinhole at the top. She knows that if a flyer has been up for a while, it will be weather-worn and the pin mark will be larger, even if it only has one. Out of the corner of her eye, she notices an elderly woman in a burgundy shaw and a black one-piece dress leaning on a homemade wooden cane.

"Lovely day isn't it," Tre hollers.

The old lady rushes down the sidewalk, stunned, as Ollie walks and stands beside Tre.

"Would you mind assisting me with a problem here, Ollie? I'm going to ask some questions, and if you don't mind repeating them for me, that would be great."

"You want me to repeat what you say?" Ollie asks with a too-cheery disposition.

"Yep. When was the last time you saw your son, Colby?"

Looking at the backs of the Morels, Ollie has never witnessed people behaving in this manner toward any law enforcement agency. He has no idea what to make of it because people are talking to him normally. The Morels say nothing. Tre nudges Ollie as the Islanders look on, amused, and interested.

"Oh…when was the last time you saw your son, Colby?" Ollie repeats.

Silence. Islanders around them chuckle. She is not giving up. Ollie leans forward and is about to ask again when Mr. Morel turns around. To his shock, they want to talk, but with him. Only him. And in Creole-French, the one language Ollie can't speak.

"Il y a trois jours (Three days ago)."

"You might want to, whip out your handy dandy notepad," Tre whispers to him.

Fumbling over, Ollie takes out his tiny notebook, leans in, and asks, "Can you repeat that?"

"La dernière fois que nous avons vu Colby, c'était il y a trois jours. Il allait bien. Il se dirigeait vers un entraînement de

15

football. (The last time we saw Colby was three days ago. He was fine. He was headed to football practice.)"

Tre responds, "Pratique du football? D'après ce que je comprends, les adolescents ne sont pas autorisés à quitter l'île - sans ou sans la permission des parents. (Football practice? From what I understand, teens are not allowed to leave the island - without or without parent's permission.)"

"I think I might have a language barrier," Ollie says.

Mr. Morel's face stays trained on Ollie, waiting patiently for him to ask another question. Tre shakes her head. She can already tell he's lying. She might as well ask questions and pick it apart later.

"Quand était-il censé être à la maison? And in English, if you don't mind. (When was he supposed to be home?)" Tre asks.

Mrs. Morel looks over her shoulder, and says, "Practice was over at nine and he was going to a friend's house, then come home, Deputy Boden."

"Who is his friend?" Tre asks.

"Who is his friend?" Ollie asks as he writes everything down.

"Matthew Crux, but when we asked, he said Colby never showed up," Mrs. Morel says.

"Say excuse me," Tre mutters under her breath.

"Please, excuse me for a minute," Ollie smiles as he and Tre step away.

"We have to make sure we find Matthew and speak to him. He's not going to talk to us unless we have his parent's permission unless Marshall Spence gives us the okay to use his office," Tre says, low to Ollie.

"Got it," Ollie says.

They step back up. The warm greeting Mr. Morel gives him makes Ollie smile, and he gets ready to write again.

"Is there anything we need to know about that night? Was

Colby acting strange, maybe he was taking something or drinking..." Tre suggests.

"Was Colby acting different, or is there anything we might need to know about his activities?"

"Our son is a good boy and happy, Deputy Boden. He wouldn't have taken up and run away from us, his friends, or the island. He was a true Islander," Mrs. Morel states as she dabs her tears.

"Unlike the current company," Mr. Morel smirks.

Ollie stops writing, and Mr. Morel wants to look at Tre but doesn't. He begins to rub his wife's back as she drops her head into her hands and starts sobbing again.

"Is there anything else, Deputy Boden?" Mr. Morel asks.

"No. But we will have to speak to you again. Thank you for your time," Tre states.

"Thank you so much for your time. I might have to speak to you again."

"My pleasure. Please don't be a stranger, Deputy Boden," Mr. Morel says, shaking Ollie's hand.

Tre and Ollie walk down the porch as the Morels turn their backs on them. Ollie looks back to see a wall of men close ranks and once again block the Morels. He follows their gaze until it lands on Tre.

"What was that? Why didn't they talk to you?" Ollie asks.

"It's a long story. Don't fall for their hospitality. It's not real. And you should have never told them you can't speak Creole-French. They'll use it against you. Always tell them to speak English, don't ask. It gives them power."

"Why would they do that when their son..."

"No, he's not just their son," Tre says as she stops. "He's one of them. We are strangers. Ollie, never show you don't know what you're doing or talking about. Rumor mills spin quickly around here. It's damaging. And believe me, I know," Tre says as she continues walking.

"Noted, Sheriff. But why—" Ollie begins.

"Therese."

A familiar male voice calls out to Tre from the distance. Turning around, Tre sees Levi Dowser rush toward her, weaving through the crowd. Levi rushes up to Tre and picks her up, holding her tight. He is dressed as a marshal and of average height with a tightly trimmed beard.

"Oh my god, Levi," Tre says loudly.

"It's been a long time."

Levi puts her down and Tre looks him up and down.

"I know. A really long time. Since when did you become the law around here?"

"I followed my father's footsteps. But Jamieson—I mean, Marshall Spence—keeps me up in the office with paperwork. He thinks anyone who doesn't know everything about Pine Island doesn't deserve to be honored with a badge."

"Or carry a weapon I guess," Tre laughs.

"Yeah, he hasn't changed. I can't believe you're here."

"Duty calls, especially when it hits my desk."

"I understand that. It's great to see you even if it's under these weird conditions."

"Weird?"

Stopping their conversation, Marshall Spence calls out for Levi.

"Levi, what in the hell… Did I radio you to stop and talk with a mainlander? No. I radioed for coffee. Simply buy, deliver, and go. Now get back to work."

"You're right. He hasn't changed. He's still a dick," Tre says.

"Yeah. Let's get the coffee together. Before you go. To catch up."

"Sorry. I don't plan on staying here longer than I have to."

Levi's face and voice drop in disappointment. It can easily be read like a chip on the shoulder.

"I don't blame you. Well, it was good to see you. You look …happy," Levi exclaims as he heads into Quills.

"Hey, Levi. Where's my brother?" Tre shouts.

"Where he always is," Levi shouts as he disappears inside.

"You have a brother?" Ollie asks, confused and shocked. He pushes his glasses back up onto his nose waiting for an answer.

"Unfortunately," Tre replies.

CHAPTER 3

THE FINKLE KIND OF SHUNNING

TRE WATCHED the gulls fly between the boats surrounding her brother's place. Small fish, whole and alive, slide down the throats of gray, white, and black herring gulls. They puff out their chests and let out an awful, loud, and rambunctious burst of laughter after barely chewing. A large colony gives way to a small one, similar to how young and old are separated. The young are socially active and have loud cries like they are bumping their chests, playing games, and finding a lifelong mate for mating season. While older, more mature gulls observe, their wings curl close to their rough-feathered bodies, and they only become moody and rowdy when disturbed. They have their own set of rules. They peck at the gelled and slimy green algae that has accumulated on the dock and boat's surfaces.

Shrimp boats bob on the choppy water on both sides of her. Most of them are faded, and the names are barely legible due to scratches, sun wear, and wire baskets with sharp corners that will easily slice a hand, which has happened. Lobster boats are hard to come by. One has a bundle of rotting lobster shells with their entrails falling into the dock puddle.

The land around the boat houses is high and dry, and the wooden boats are stumpy compared to the schooners beside them. Makeshift boxes are decorated in green, blue, yellow, and white, with the signature in cursive half moving in the slight breeze that blows past the houseboats. Few have large, black, and wiry nets in the middle, trapping bugs and rats— not ideal for those who live there, who are terrified of being able to enter the cabin through the open sliding door.

The plywood on one expensive houseboat appears in good condition, but on the other side, it's low in the water, making a strange, muddy moan as the steel scrapes along the edge of another boat. Satellites move not because of speed or signal. But because of the lovely hollow wind blowing over the rusted stains left by the rain.

As Tre places her hand against the boat's rail and the door frame, unmusical and tattling tunes, flat spoons, and forks collide. The chimes unhook from the shoulder and land on the boat's floor with a dead lyric. She stops by pulling the halfway sliding door open the rest of the way.

—————

Tre walks in and finds herself in the living room. Or what most people would call a trash dump with living creatures raising families. She rubs her eyes. She hasn't even been on the island for eight hours, and she can feel the migraine coming and reaching around her head, gnawing, and scratching at her temples.

In front of her, a small loveseat looks to be cut, poorly at best, in half. The stitching is terrible, with cotton and guts poking out. The light shines through the dirty windowpane, revealing the sticky leftover black liquid inside, leaving a ring on the table. There are empty beer cans lining the path to the sink like a racetrack leading up to empty Tequila and vodka bottles on the counters and dirty dishes overflowing in the sink.

From the back comes a long, deep snore. She leans in and

looks inside the master bedroom, which most people would describe as a hole-in-the-wall shithole. Others would classify it as a claustrophobic tissue box.

"You gotta be kidding me," Tres says, sighing.

Finkle is out cold and on his stomach as Tre walks over to a small wooden end table and lifts the handle of a coal-colored electric lantern. She looks around, and lanterns are placed near the kitchen's medium-sized windows and scattered throughout the living room, three to a corner. Everything is set too high, the LED lights inside are bright, and the knob is completely turned up. His boots are unlaced with a blanket draped across his dark-colored jeans, his arm dead on the floor, and his back to the wall. He snores once more.

"Jacob John Finkle," Tre yells.

Startled, Finkle jumps up and hits the back of his head on the low frame. The thump is harsh and unexpected. He rolls back onto his stomach, burying his face in the soiled covers and moaning in agony. Tre steps forward as Finkle squirms and rubs his head. Tre kicks the empty beer cans, disgusted.

"Ever hear of cleaning, Jacob?" Tre demands, looking at him as he crawls to a sitting position.

"The maid has the year off. And it's Finkle. Just Finkle," he mutters as he pushes himself up to a sitting position.

Finkle staggers out and into the kitchen, still rubbing the back of his head. He shields his eyes from the sun beaming in as Tre cocks her hip, resting her hand on the duty belt. He opens the refrigerator to see nothing except a rotten loaf of bread and moldy cheese. He slams the door causing the fridge to rock on the uneven floor.

"My god, Jacob. You look like hell ran over you. Twice," Tre tells him.

He walks a few steps, crawls over the loveseat, plops down, and says, "Do you ever knock?"

"I would have, but the snoring would have drowned it out."

Finkle looks down and flings around some beer cans with his hand, picks one up, and shakes it. It's empty. He drops it and picks up another. It's empty, and he once again drops it. The third one is shaken. The beer inside sloshes around and puts a smile on Finkle's face.

"Third time's the charm," Finkle says as he sits back and sips it.

It's not the best-tasting thing in the world, but it'll suffice as she curls her lips and pulls her head back into her neck in disgust.

"Jacob..."

Finkle, his mouth full of beer, holds out the can with his hand and wags his fingers as he swallows. It's flat and weak. There's not much to taste except the aluminum of the can. Not the best, but he's not letting it go.

"No. No. I don't go by Jacob."

"Since when?"

"It's been about, oh, eighteen years," Finkle informs her.

"Are you kidding me?"

"I'm not. I needed to make a change, so I did."

"That's not a change."

"It was for me, at least. In fact, I doubt anyone remembers my given name," Finkle says while holding the beer can to his lips.

Tre sighs, knowing that everyone knows who he is. He's difficult to forget, no matter how hard one tries.

"Maybe you should ask," Tre suggests.

Finkle leans forward at Tre's suggestion, smiling as he tosses the beer can behind him. "I think I might do that. But what I'm curious about is why you're here," Finkle asks, his eyes narrowing.

"Work."

Confusion falls across Finkle's face. "What work?"

"Colby Morel is missing."

Tre is transfixed by Finkle's reaction to her, which isn't

much. At first. Either his hangover is booming down on him, or his sheer stupidity and guilt are something he's learned to live with. Tre notices as he taps his dirty, oil-stained fingers on top of his knee. He increased his breathing and licked his lips nervously.

"You wouldn't know anything about that now. Would you?"

"Me? No," he says as he stands, shaking his head.

Finkle steps through the trail of cans, back to the refrigerator, and pops his head back in. Tre bites her bottom lip as she stares out the window at the water. A filthy white satellite trawler spins and blows its horn as it approaches the water. The horn's sound shakes the little houseboat.

"Don't lie to me."

"I'm not," Finkle replies.

He pokes his head over the refrigerator, fakes a smile, and disappears back inside it. His hand tightens around the handle. Tre catches the large drums out of the corner of her eyes. And each one was stuffed to the brim with shrimp and fish.

"I'm not lying. Check my schedule if you don't believe me."

"I didn't say you were, and I intend to," Tre says.

"Then why are you asking?"

"Because it's my job, Jacob. How long do plan on staring in that thing?"

"As long as it takes for you to get the hint and go away."

Finkle's cold attitude doesn't make Tre uncomfortable at all. She expected it, just not in the drunken or hungover way.

"You want me to leave?"

"Finkle shuts the fridge, looks at her and says, "I know I'm not alone in thinking this. But yeah. I want you to leave. You don't belong here anymore."

Tre can't believe what Finkle is saying. Being turned

against or ignored by Islanders is one thing. But by your own brother, she never saw it coming, even after all these years.

"Sorry, Jacob. I can't do that. I came here to do a job and I'm going to do it."

"No one is going to help you. Islanders aren't interested in forgiveness, or have you forgotten after all these years?" Finkle asks, leaning against the small counter that separates them. Smiling, he places his face in his hands.

Tre begins to step toward the front door with a chuckle, and says, "I don't care."

"I would. People around here have become quieter and closer over the last few years, well eighteen years, since you've been here. Things just aren't the same," Finkle checks his watch. "It doesn't mean a thing when it comes to one of their own. Besides, isn't it Sunday, shouldn't you be in church or something? I mean, isn't that what mainlanders do?"

Finkle closes his eyes, shakes his head, and looks up as Tre steps halfway out the front door.

"Sunday?" Tre asks.

"Yep."

Tre steps out the door. Then turns back around to see Finkle leering at her like he has a leg up. She smirks and shakes her head.

"It's Wednesday, dipshit."

"Wed-Wednesday?"

It's been three days since Finkle came face to face with the gel, the drool that fell in front of his eyes. The streetlights busted and the crunch of the bulbs.

"Thanks for the warm welcome home," Tre says.

Tre walks off. The sound of her boots stomping on the dock fades and Finkle drops his head in his hands.

He hadn't been asleep in three days.

While Ollie is scribbling in his notebook, the boat's driver peeks over his shoulder. Catching him, Ollie brings his notebook to the middle of his chest. Both become distracted when they hear someone barging down the dock quickly. It's Tre. By the furrow of her brows and the purse of her lips, Ollie can tell she's not happy.

"It's time to go, Ollie," Tre says.

As she walks past, she unties the rope, tosses it inside, and descends into the rowboat. Unsurprised, the driver turns his head away from her. Marshall Spence nods his head like a man in a tower, staring at them for nearly seven seconds before smiling like he just won the blue ribbon in a pie-eating contest. Preferably a shit pie if Tre could decide.

"I hate this place."

Ollie shifts back and forth, twisting at the waist, trying to figure out what is going on. Marshall Spence is patted on the shoulder by one of his deputies as the tall man digs his rubber boots into the sand and walks away. He looked over his shoulder again before cracking a half-grin.

"Ollie," Tre says, sternly.

Ollie steps in clumsily. The boat wavers in the water. Tre, rolling her eyes, grabs Ollie's arm, settles him, and he sits. The driver takes off immediately, and Ollie falls backward in the boat. When the boat's bow hits the small waves, it bobs up and down violently with each one. Ollie tries to get back into his seat. Tre returns her gaze towards the shore and dock as each person is shrinking the further, she gets, except for one.

Finkle watches her as he leans on his leg on a rock. Tre's wild hair wraps around her face as she stares at Finkle as he chugs the rest of his beer. Whether they like it or not, they will always be siblings. Unfortunately, what one does affects the other, and they are both aware of this. But for them, it's not just psychically and emotionally. But, socially, the one thing you can have on the island that sets you apart from the others. Tre's departure ruined the Finkle name, and he was the wrong one to repair it.

Finkle takes a deep breath in as he notices residents closely watching him, not for entertainment but for business. They want to see if he reacts to seeing Tre, such as rage, turning away, or hatred. Finkle keeps his mouth shut in front of everyone as if Finkle wants to project himself onto Tre. With a snicker, he cheers his beer to them, then returns his attention to Tre as she disappears on her way back to the mainland. In his hand, he crushes the can.

"Bitch," he says, throwing it her way. The Islanders stare, laugh, nod their heads, and a few applaud his reaction.

Tre turns to Pine Island, closes her eyes, and takes a deep breath.

Finkle turns the steps off the rocks and looks at the residents. They give a wave of approval as Finkle flashes them a quick smile. He quickens his shuffle across the street and through a line of children walking in a straight line down the road. To the children, their jubilant smiles never fail to flaunt their joy and excitement at seeing another islander as Finkle disappears into the small woods.

CHAPTER 4
MAINLANDER TRE

A SUGARY POWDER floats from the mouth of Tonya, the Terrebonne Parish Sheriff's Department secretary. With her sharp, glossy nails she takes a bite of the donut. She licks her lips, smearing her pink lipstick.

The phone rings off the hook, and she slips another donut onto her curved finger, hoping not to drop it. Some people believe that donuts are the best friends of the police. For Tonya, donuts are her middle name. Swinging her hips around the end of the desk, she falls into her chair, picks up the receiver, and picks at her donut. Tre and Ollie walk through the double glass door. Tre is talking fast as Ollie is writing in his notepad, trying to keep up.

"I want you to dig and find out whatever you can about Colby. Friends, family, likes, dislikes – everything. Even social media," Tre stops at the front desk. Tonya waves with the powered-coated fingers as Tre begins to go through the mail. Ollie looks confused.

"I'll call the parents to see if he they know of any accounts."

"No. They won't."

"How do you know that?"

Tre continues to go through the pile of mail, smirking and shaking her head.

"Easy. It's against what they teach. Besides, he's a teen. And every teen has an account of some kind. Just look for it."

"Google will help," Tonya butts in.

"Listen to the maven of Instagram. Try initials, his last name first, that kind of stuff," Tre tells him.

Tonya hangs up, and says, "Here's the file you asked for about Jacob."

"But what if I can't find anything? Should I call Marshall Spence?"

"No. Never call him without checking with me first. He might give you the runaround and besides, he's already pinned you. So, best to leave him alone."

"Jacob has been a busy little bee." Tonya rubs her nails together.

Tre flips through the file quickly, and says, "Why am I not surprised?" She closes the file. "Well, I was hoping to get at least a week, hell, a day into this case before he popped up. Ollie, let me know what you find."

"You also have a visitor. Waiting in your office."

"Who?"

"He told me not to tell you."

"This day just keeps getting better. If you find anything else, let me know. Especially when it comes to my brother. Ollie, use a computer. Not your phone."

Tre takes a step back and begins walking backward from the front desk to her office. Ollie comes to a halt as Tonya motions to his phone.

"Searching on the phone is easier."

"You heard her."

Tre is standing outside her office door. She hesitates for a second, stares at her nameplate on the door, and takes a deep breath. She's nervous, as evidenced by her puffy cheeks. She clenches Finkle's file in hand, and she walks in.

"Elliot. I hadn't expected you. What a delightful surprise!" Tre tries her hardest to act, but it doesn't work.

"Cut the shit, Tre."

"Good morning to you as well."

Captain Elliot Amant is the quintessential blue-collar man in his sixties, not to mention a midlife crisis that included hair plugs that look worse than an untrimmed wig. He sighs as he fiddles with his tie, smoothing it down while attempting to maintain his calm and professional demeanor, which is nonexistent. He's been an asshole ever since Tre became Sheriff.

"You know why I am here," he says, turning toward her.

"No, I don't," Tre says as she approaches her desk, drops the mail, and sits down.

"Oh, give me a break. Tre, we both know anything could have happened to that kid. Especially if he left in the middle of the night."

"There's only one way off the island. It's still sitting at the dock, and has been there for a very long time."

"Maybe he or someone else did the same thing you did all those years ago and came to the mainland."

Elliot tosses his hat on Tre's desk, knocking over the pencil holder, and moving some loose papers around. Tre watches as one floats down onto the floor, and says, "That's impossible."

She turns to him as he rubs his index finger across his lips, thinking as he looks around the room. Eventually, his eyes land on Tre who is smiling.

"Really? And how can you be sure?"

"Simple. No one in town dares say my name. Hell, they don't even acknowledge my existence. Ask Ollie if you want, he was the go-to between me and them."

Elliot throws his hands in the air, slams them down on the chair's arms, and says, "Well, if I have to depend on Ollie, let's just throw the entire case in the bayou with gators. No, I know, how about I go on TV and tell them Ollie is handling everything? Not to mention, his Creole is non-existent."

"Are you done yet?"

"No, I'm not," Elliot says as he stands and walks around the office, "I have the district attorney breathing down my neck."

Tre is baffled She shakes her head and clears her throat. Elliot paces and places his fingers in the corner of his eyes. He stops and squeezes them.

"Why are y'all so interested in getting this case closed so fast? I just opened it."

"You know why."

"Remind me."

Tre leans back in her chair and folds her arms. Her lifted brows say a lot to Elliot as he sighs and stares back at her. He is speechless for a few minutes as Tre watches him gather the right words to explain the speediness and quietness of the matter.

"I know this is not what you want to hear. But Pine Island is one of the wealthiest islands we have. Not to mention, it's the only one inhabitable. That means a lot to this state."

"You mean you want tourism."

"Yes, tourism."

"And what makes you think the Islanders will want to have flashes from cameras in their faces all the time, sell keychains, and pose for pictures with people like Bob, who wear Louisiana shirts and fanny packs around their waists?"

"It doesn't matter. It's not their choice."

"Like hell it is. I might not be there anymore, but I know the council still has to pass the bill. And I know damn well, it's not going to happen. They aren't like the mainliners, they have their own set of rules, laws, and standards. If the state or

31

parish didn't want that, maybe you should have stopped them a long time ago."

"Solve it, Tre. Do whatever you have to do, get whatever you have to get, and call in whomever you have to. Just figure out what is happening on that island."

Tre sits up, and says, "It's not that simple, Elliot. I can't just snap my fingers and have all the answers you want. Those people are not like you and me. They aren't normal."

"They are normal, Tre. You don't want them to be."

"They aren't," Tre yells. She stands and walks around to the front of her desk.

"You left a long time ago, so leave all your personal feelings aside and solve the case. Cases. In fact, I'm going to help you with it."

Elliot steps around her. He scoops his hat up and places it on his head. He straightens it in front of Tre and waits. He's making her sweat this one. He's enjoying her squirm. But she never saw what was about to happen next.

"I was talking to the janitor, and he said he noticed a stale odor coming from one of the offices. Come to think of it; I can smell something. It could be dangerous, and I wouldn't want anything to happen to my team."

"Wait."

"Due to unforeseen circumstances, this building is closed. The sign will be on tomorrow and I will have to make sure you do your job evidently until it's back open. Per the health department rules and regulations. Which means you need a place where you can always have access to potential evidence, places, and witnesses while working."

"What are you doing?"

Elliot opens the door, looks back at her, and says, "Tonya will be here. In another location that is."

"Elliot."

"Pack your bags, Tre. You're going home."

As Elliot shuts the door, Tre nervously looks around.

Anxiety begins to bubble deep inside her gut, crawling and inching its way up and tickling her esophagus. To avoid screaming, she rakes everything off her desk. Papers fly in the air, mail covers the ground, and her desk phone hits the floor with a ding, along with her pens and pencils. When her nameplate thuds to the ground, she bends down to pick it up.

She stops. Her hand trembles violently. She grabs it with one hand and brings it close to her chest, turning pale and breathing heavily.

A neon "five o'clock somewhere" sign points to a stocked open bar. A pink outline of a woman's butt glows outside the door with the bar's name lit in blue: The Blue Oyster.

A few bikers play darts. They cheer each other on as they prepare to throw, but yell at each other to mess up right before they throw, guessing with anticipation. The walls are covered with Mardi Gras masks with dates underneath, dating from the 1980s to the present. From the neon signs surrounding them, some of the masks, which are red, black, purple, long-nosed, small, and petite, glisten and shimmer.

A busty waitress in a white halter top walks through the crowd in too-tight black pants that show the lining of her underwear, carrying a tray full of bottled beer from the bar. After being slapped on the buttocks by one man and whistled at by a few other men, she hopes to get a large tip if she flirts a little harder. She walks up to the back pool table, drops off two fresh beers, and picks up the empty ones as she walks away.

Blue dust swirls out when you twist the chalk on the pool stick. The pool stick moves slowly across the table, eventually reaching the green carpet. Tre aims, gliding it through her slender frame, and the tip inches away from the white ball. She hits it, and the balls in the pyramid speed up and roll everywhere. The number four ball finds its way into the corner pocket, while the number seven ball finds its way into the middle pocket to the left.

"Lucky shot."

Tre raises her head to look at Philip Jones before hitting another ball into the pocket. Philip is one of her deputies, with black hair cut high and tight and clean-shaven. He's athletic and quick on his feet. Tre's gaze returns. She wouldn't normally mix business and pleasure, but for him, she doesn't mind, at least until things get too complicated.

Mornings are uncomplicated. Get out of bed, dress, avoid small talk, or gather around a hot cup of coffee. Both parties benefit from this arrangement. Tre scuffs and tears the dirty and dingy fabric of the pool table. She tosses the stick on the table, and Philip sighs in relief because, as usual, he is losing.

"Forget it," Tre exclaims as she grabs her beer, downs it, and grabs another from the tray as the waitress passes. The waitress doesn't notice.

"Whoa. Slow down. It's not a race," Philip says as he brings his beer to his mouth.

"Everything is a race. And always will be," Tre says, in between breaths.

Tre flops down and waves her hand to the bartender. She doesn't have to say what she wants. It's an automatic, silent request. "Tre" equals peanuts in the bowl; a pool table is always open. There's an endless supply of smooth, chilled tap beer. Philip swivels around and places his elbows on the bar as Tre snaps open peanuts from a small, cheap brown basket.

Tre avoids his gaze. He breathes in loudly and holds up his finger for a beer. Each is served with an open-top and a shot glass by the bartender. He flips the bottle of vodka in the air, fills the shot glasses, and then sets the bottle in front of them.

"What's this for?" Tre asks.

"Call it compliments of the house. My house," Philip says, handing her a shot glass.

They shoot it. Tre's eyes open, and she puckers her lips letting out a whoop through her puffed cheeks. Philip slams the shot glass upside on the table, shakes his head, and loosens his tongue.

"Now that hits the spot. Want another one?" Philip asks.

"Oh, yeah," Tre agrees.

They throw back three more shots with the first one's glasses still on the bar's counter. The warmth of the liquor descends on Philip, and he takes a deep breath in to cool down. Tre smiles as she dips her fingers in the drops her upside-down glass created. Philip sets them up for another shot.

"So, he's sending you back."

"Jesus, Philip. Why don't you say something a little more interesting to get me in bed before I re-enter hell?"

"Come on, it can't be that bad."

"You have no idea."

Focused on the oblong-shaped peanut, Tre twirls it, listening to Philip ramble, but his words sound like someone screaming into a glass. She rubs her fingers around the boiled shell before she cracks it. The sound echoes around her as she picks another and another. She drops the large cardboard-tasting hearts of the peanuts back in the basket and the brittle, splintery body around it. She shifts her eyes to her left.

She sees Philips's mouth moving, his lips wet as he looks at her with a half-sided smile and lifts his eyebrows before taking another shot. She returns to the last few peanuts in the basket. Toward the bottom, the peanuts shatter easily in her hand like Styrofoam.

Philip calls out to the bartender, but Tre doesn't hear much except the sip of beer left in his bottle, rattling inside as he shakes it. The customer's shoes shuffle on the dirty floor, and the sharp end of a dart hits the target, embedding it into the soft game board.

One left. It's large but thin. One end has prickles of wood at the butt of it, which Tre has never seen. Maybe it's because it was at the bottom of the bag, or the sun faded it. Tre cracks it.

Black oil flows and covers her fingers. It's unusually rotten if a peanut can be rotten. The smell is gut-wrenching like fly-covered fish heads in a barrel, and as she pulls her fingers apart, the gel latches on and hugs her skin with a slimy, raw coating as if it's kissing her hello. She quickly picks up the small square napkin from under her beer bottle where condensation has accumulated. Everything around her is hurling down a tunnel of her loneliness and back to reality.

"This could be a good thing, Tre."

Tre, disgusted, tosses the black-stained napkin onto the counter and frowns at Philip. He understands her situation and why she left Pine Island in the first place. But he suggests it's a good thing. He must be drunk.

"Why don't you have a few more shots and then tell me that again."

"I'm serious. Maybe they have changed. You did." Tre laughs as Philip keeps talking. "Time heals all wounds."

Tre leans against the counter, her hand mocking Philip as she bats her eyes and gives him an airheaded stare, wide-open eyes distant and ditzy,. She imagines Philip's wife looked like this when he spoke, sharing his wisdom on life before she left him for the greasy, skinny mechanic who fixed her car every other day at the shop, at the only hotel in town, and their house four times a week.

"Please. Enlighten me oh wise one. Give me your wisdom on island life."

Philip stops. He notices Tre's hair blowing between her ears as she slowly moves her head back and forth. Philip sighs. He's uncomfortable. He tries to drink his beer, but he can't, she's watching every move he makes with curiosity and awe.

"Okay. Okay. I get it. I have no idea what island life is like."

"Thank you," Tre says.

Getting up, she waves at the bartender. He nudges his head towards the door. Payment isn't needed when it comes to Tre. She pays her tab at the end of the month. The bar was her first job. Where most would never take on an islander, she proved she wasn't your typical one. She worked hard to save enough money for her first apartment and school due to the tips and overtime she did every weekend.

She learned a lot about the world she was kept away from. How were women supposed to be treated? Everyday education, such as math and driving. After a few years on the mainland, she realized she wasn't being protected by her parents, but rather kept away from the real world. She was taught that the island would shield her from harm. In turn, it did the opposite. Leaving that place freed her.

Now she must return to the place which almost ruined her. In the back of her mind, placed in a compartment with a lock and key, is the fear she might become part of their twisted traditions again.

The wind off the waterfront swirls around them as Tre and Philip walk outside the swinging door and past a few new customers. Philip loses his balance. Tre grabs him by the arm, pulls him closer, and he falls into her.

Breathing heavily, he pushes her burnt chocolate-colored hair back and places it behind her ear to see her smooth and creamy skin. Tre looks at him with her cinnamon-brown eyes to see his thirsty and villainous stare. She knows what he is thinking.

"At ease, big boy."

"Come on, Tre. You and I both know we need this, A stress reliever."

Philip wraps his hands around her waist, gripping the back of her shirt, and teases her neck with his lips, leaving his hot breath to linger on her skin.

"Unfortunately, I still have to go in the morning."

Tempting, but Tre still turns it down as she slips from his arms and walks around him. He drops his head down and chuckles.

"At least let me go with you," Philip says.

Singing and hanging all over each other, a group of drunken men walk out happy and willing to share their foul-smelling breath with anyone willing to listen or join in.

"Can't. Ollie is already coming," Tre replies.

Shocked and disappointed, Philip places his hands on his hips and leans toward her. The men sing louder, becoming annoying.

"Ollie? All he does is take notes," Philip reminds her.

"That's why I'm bringing him," Tre tells him, twisting around.

She smiles and blows a kiss to him as she turns around.

"Better do something about this before it gets out of hand," Tre suggests. She points to the men as they wobble in the growing space between them. Philip doesn't care. He never takes his eyes off Tre.

"They're fine. Will I get to see you before you leave?" he shouts, trying to be louder than the singing.

Tre rolls her eyes. What they have is supposed to be simple, vague, and merely basic. Philip is overbearing and stubborn about her leaving like he's a protector. She has had enough of those in her lifetime. The only person she needs is herself. The men walk around Philip, arms over his shoulders, and he smiles with them as they sway back and forth.

"Come on. Sing with us," a drunk biker says.

"No, I'm good. How about you head back inside and try out that karaoke machine," Philip says.

"Don't forget to water my plants and talk to them every day," Tre shouts.

"Plants. Yes. Got it," Philip yells as the bikers block him from Tre. "Tre, hold up."

"And keep Elliot off my ass until I figure out what's going on."

"That I can't promise. But I'll try. Be careful."

"Quit acting like we're a couple. It's creepy," Tre twists back around and walks down the sidewalk.

"I'm just showing concern for my sheriff," Philip shouts.

"Yeah. Night Deputy," Tre shouts back, putting her arm in the air. She slowly disappears the further she goes.

CHAPTER 5

PINE ISLAND, SICKLED AND SLICED

A SICKLE-SHAPED PIECE of land can be seen from the sky and in the plane's single pilot's eyes. Straight like the handle, the island's base, and where the docks meet the water —not a canal, river, or lake—because the closer you get to the island, the more it opens up, the more the town is exposed. As things stand, Mother Nature is to blame and has always been held accountable for what happened to the land splitting, according to the Islanders. Due to the hatred of mainlanders, the two communities are separate. At first, it wasn't mutual.

In 1858, mainlanders were minding their own business, strolling in and out of the local and best grocery store. Children ran down the street, laughing as they teased a collie named Fido with a ball, letting him close. But never let him catch it. Men and women fill the streets, sometimes separating, men at the saloon and women at the local store window as if they are shopping. But each stop to hang out on the porch of the bar or sidewalk. It's when they hear a friend talk about the poker game last night, or how Martha was drinking and babbling about her marriage problems. That's when the issue would begin within the group and family.

On a crisp, clear, cloudless summer day, the sun burned

down on the mainlander's shoulders. Darkness blanketed the sky, engulfing and swallowing the light as the wind lifted the wooden posts from the ground, tossing them into the street. Doors to the busy saloon rip off the hinges and end up on the ground.

Families huddled together in the church at the end of the street. Big enough for the mainlanders but small enough to feel the shake and tug of the wind as it taps on the windows and bangs in the welcome doors. Hands clasped, heads down, and praying, they are frightened and nervous. There hasn't been a storm as powerful as the one raging across the Atlantic in a long time, complete with a black streak of lightning. A streak of light cuts through the sky and lands in the heart of town. As it travels down the street, the ground bubbles and explodes around the town, spitting out the dirt as if it is either hungry or thirsty for something more than dryness.

The rumble of the land cracks, sending a small portion of Louisiana's tip into the Mississippi River and out to 426 small islands most are inhabitable with the exception of two. One, covered with lush green topped pine trees and people on the mainland, while the second, broken and settled across is a shattered church ravaged by bloody, dismembered bodies and quiet voices in shock of those who are being sent into oblivion miles away from loved ones, friends, and land. It grows further and further away from their eyes.

The island is 25 miles away in all directions. In any case, it is more self-sufficient and livable than in the past. Throughout the island, wildlife freely wanders alongside Islanders who explore its beauty and promise.

The town was never officially named. Mainlanders refer to it as Pine Island, while Islanders sent there call it home.

On a large two-wheeled green suitcase, Ollie rolls on the pavement while the left wheel shakes as if it's about to pop off. He knows he should pick it up, but it would be easier to have one hand free in case something catches his interest. And that could be easy as he looks around, constantly adjusting his black backpack straps. The pavement always looks freshly poured without the white or yellow lines separating the left from the right, the comings and goings, and the shoulder for safety. Tall trees stand on either side, and their branches are full and lush, like an oil painting left in a summer shower.

The tip tops sway back and forth in the wind as Ollie and Tre feel the crisp, cool fall weather on their cheeks and through their hair. Tre only has one, in hand, Tre grips a large tan duffle bag and nothing else. Most women have multiple bags: one for their clothes, shoes that match their outfits, makeup that can be glam or dark depending on the occasion, and accessories.

Recently, she hasn't been around the island's peacefulness, especially during the day. It looks different from the other side. Still, a shiver runs up her spine. The night was always so dark, silent, and disturbing. Beneath it all, Tre always felt like The Unquiet was speaking to her. Once she left, she turned the television on so loudly that her neighbors banged on the opposite side of the wall or called the cops. It is funny they did that, because she is a cop.

Towards the middle of the sickle, the road is winding and sharp. The distant noise of an engine turns the corner, accelerating at Tre and Ollie. The game of cat and mouse isn't fair when the mice barely notice the smell of decay, it was there and then gone before they could blink. Ollie stumbles forward as Tre drops her duffle, lifting spare leaves still turning yellow, red, and pale green.

A white bronco with the sign Marshall on the side, sitting on a green streak, speeds past, glossing the side doors. There are no blue or red lights, or a siren speaker attached to the top or sides. The driver could be a couple of people. Tre, on the other hand, suspects it's Marshall Spence. He tried everything he could to keep her away as soon as he found out she was returning to stay and investigate. He eventually failed. Although, she wishes he had won for many reasons other than selfishness on both their parts. A sickle's middle is deep, curved, and sharp. Its tires squeal as it fades from sight.

"Do you think they mistook us?" Ollie inquires, looking over Tre's shoulder.

"Ask me after you've been here a few days," Tre says.

"Do you think they're coming back?" Ollie says, shrugging.

"Not for you," Tre informs him.

"We're the good guys."

Tre shakes her head and says, "You are." Tre slings her duffle over her shoulder and continues walking. Ollie grabs his suitcase and proceeds to follow.

"Hey, Sheriff. Can I ask you a question?"

"Shoot."

Ollie's suitcase stalls in the crack in the dock, but Tre continues. He jerks it open, almost falling over. He quickens his steps.

"I was talking to… well the rumors at the station… I mean…"

Stopping short, Tre turns to Ollie, who is taken off guard as he bumps into her. He steps back, embarrassed, and nervous. He drops his head and barely looks at her. He never, in his whole three-and-a-half-year career, touched Tre, let alone got that close to her. She stares at him. He sees Tre's brow furrow. Her lips thin out as she folds them in and over her teeth, and her knuckles turn white as she tightens her grip on the duffle's handle.

"And what did you hear?" Tre asks.

Ollie clears his throat, and says, "Um, Philip was talking about it. You don't have to tell me if you don't want to."

"It's not any of yours or anyone else's at the station business. But if you must know, I am from here, but left a long time ago. That's all you need to know."

Tre continues walking as Ollie watches and says, "Is it true that was eight years ago?"

"Ollie, we are here to find Colby Morel. And when we do, it's over and we leave. Now we have to get to the house before the sun goes down."

"But that's hours away," Ollie says, confused.

"The rate this is going with that bag of yours, it's going to take that long. Better pick it up," Tre instructs. Birds sing a haunting song around them while they keep walking.

Tre ramps up her pace as she passes a dark hole on her left, but Ollie takes a breather. A strong breeze blows from a roadside archway made of trees and hits Ollie in the face, nearly knocking him over on the pine-lined dirt road. It has a foul odor, like eggs that have been left out in the sun for too long. Another gust of wind swirls the dirt in front of him as if examining him. He is immobile.

He watches as the pale hand of a female emerges and hovers in the shadows, never touching the daylight. The hand is slender, delicate, and inviting. He can hear the grinding of the bones. On the outside, goosebumps slowly pop up and cover his arms as he feels something crawling up his leg. Its steps, like needle pricks, make him flinch the deeper they dig. But nothing is there, and he can't look down to check. He tilts his head in pain as the ringing in his ears grows louder, piecing the eardrums as they pop and split. oldness kisses his ear as he closes his eyes, intently listening, swaying back and forth as it whispers his name in a seductive and erotic voice.

"Hey."

Startled, Ollie twists to see Tre looking at him as he follows her arm to her hand on his shoulder. Ollie turns his head back to the archway. His skin begins to warm up; the kisses he was feeling dissipates into nothingness, and the disgusting smell vanishes. Feeling a bulge in his pants, he quickly covers it the best he can with his hand and suitcase.

"Are you alright? Ollie?"

"Did you… Nothing. It was nothing. I just got lost."

"You're in the same spot where I left you?"

Tre watches as Ollie tries not to look at the dark archway, glaring at his side eye. But he's not doing a good job of hiding it.

"I warned you that this place would get under your skin. Come on ."

Ollie walks bow-legged to catch up with Tre. In the darkness, pine needles fall to the ground as a pair of worn, scratched black boots step further into the darkness and continue to follow them.

Ollie walks alongside Tre as he battles the ground while rolling his suitcase, dropping it every few seconds. Tre comes to a standstill and places her foot on a broken half-buried post. Ollie appears and pushes his black-rimmed glasses up the bridge of his nose, causing sweat to fall against the sides of his nose.

"There it is," Tre says.

"What?" Ollie inquires.

Through her pursing lips, Tre relentingly responds. "Home."

He looks through his semi-foggy glasses, and everything looks like a kaleidoscope, especially the two-story house nestled in the open field surrounded by pine trees. Its upper windows have white and clean frames. The top chimney is dark and tall, with a short, stubby chimney end hanging out. On either side of the dark blue door with a silver handle are two bay windows. The wraparound porch has a light red dusting, red posts, and light-colored wooded steps.

"Wow. It's incredible."

"It is, indeed."

"Do your parents know we're on our way?"

"Nope."

"Didn't you call them?"

"Why would I?"

"I always call my parents. I have a reminder on my phone."

"Really? Interesting."

She looks ahead, her hand on her trembling knees. She nods, pumping herself up to take the next step as if swallowing an acorn. Ollie never takes his gaze away from the house while muttering to himself.

"Perhaps we should stay in a hotel."

"On the island, there are none and there never will be."

Tre throws her duffle bag over her shoulder and looks at Ollie.

"Let's get this over with, Ollie. We're burning daylight."

Ollie sprints the rest of the way across the field to catch up.

Ollie is a few steps behind Tre as they walk toward what she perceives to be impending doom. She has no idea what to expect, but whatever happens, happens. She is far from prepared, especially when it comes to her dad.

———

Tre never said goodbye. She was already gone when her parents and Finkle finally woke up. It was the only thing she ever regretted as she stole her father's rowboat and vanished, vowing never to return. She traveled through the dense white fog that covered her mouth as she made her way to the mainland, tears streaming down her cheeks. She was steadfast and never wavered in her decision. As hard as it was deep down, she knew she had made the right choice. She couldn't stay there and lead the life they wanted her to. She wanted and needed more. And so, she left.

Now standing at a freshly painted door, she shakes her head. What is going to happen? What are her parents going to say? Will they embrace her? Strikes of nervous electricity rush through her veins, tingling her fingertips. Swallowing hard as if a chuck of coal Santa left for her got rammed down her throat, she feels Ollie stare. He's waiting for her to do something. Being the sheriff she is on the mainland, she shakes it off, sticks out her chest, but not too far, and turns the knob. Straightening her back, she holds her chin high before reaching for the newly gleaming silver knob.

It easily unlatches, and she slowly opens it with a loud creak.

Light shines through the crack she's made into the foyer, illuminating the walls covered in small, medium, and large frames. In-between the frames there are few open spots on the wall where frames used to hang. An old washing basin with a blue ring around its white curved edges; a pitcher crowned blue like the front; white flowers painted along the S-shaped handle; and pure white hand towels perfectly folded next to it with the initial "F" in cursive toward the bottom. Above it is a dusty oblong shape with a dark outline, and the panel behind it is spotless.

Tre enters and carefully places her bag near the front door. She walks further inside, light on her feet, and looks to the right, then to the left. She takes a long, deep breath, closes her eyes to regain the courage she had before leaving, and licks her lips. Ollie slams the door as she opens her eyes. She spins around.

"Well, if they didn't know we were here before, they do now," Tre exhales, disappointed.

"I didn't do it, I swear. Something yanked out of my hand. Must have been the wind," Ollie says.

"Honestly, Ollie, I thought you'd come up with something better than wind," Tre responds.

"Oh, don't be too hard on him. Who knows what it is anymore?" a female voice says.

Tre and Ollie turn to see a short, silver-haired woman in a blue maid's uniform staring at them as she wipes her hand on her white apron. Sabine has been with the Finkle family since she was a young girl, and she is now sixty-four years old. Mrs. Finkle was gracious enough to take Sabine in and give her a job so she wouldn't have to leave the island for the mainland. Tre gives her a friendly smile.

"Sabine."

Sabine embraces Tre and rubs her hand on her back as she holds her close. Tre closes her eyes and returns to the tight hugs she has given her since she can remember. It's one of the things she's missed since moving away. They take a step back and look at each other.

"Miss Therese, it's been a long time."

"Did you shrink?"

Tre smiles and notices Ollie standing in the background, pushing his glasses up the bridge of his nose as Sabine waves her off. As he trips over his suitcase and nearly falls to the ground, Tre tilts her head like she's watching a slow-moving car crash. Finally, balancing himself, Ollie pulls himself together and clears his throat. Sabine leans in close to Tre.

"What an interesting young man. Please tell me he's your boyfriend, or dare I say it, your fiancé."

"No, and no."

"He's handsome."

"Sabine, this is Deputy Ollie Boden. We work together on the mainland."

"Oh, the mainland. Well, now. Nice to meet you, Deputy Boden. I'm Sabine, the house everything as I like to say."

Ollie reaches out his hand and shakes Sabine's vigorously. She smiles as she feels her arm moving up and down like a continuous wave hitting rocks.

"Nice to meet you, ma'am."

"A deputy and manners. Two things I like in a man."

Tre breathes in the pleasing and sweet aroma of something familiar. Closing her eyes, she follows it, along with her stomach, towards the charcoal antique oven against the wall in the kitchen.

"I know, I know, you don't have to tell me twice. It's about ready to come out," Sabine tells her.

"I have missed it. But I think I need to see my parents first before I make myself at home."

Sabine takes Ollie by the hand and begins to lead him into the kitchen.

"Come on young man," Sabine tells Ollie.

Tre looks toward the study far down the hall, cuts her eyes upstairs, and even out around the corner to the back door as Ollie bumps her while being dragged toward the kitchen.

"So, where are they, Sabine?"

"Have you ever had fresh bread?" Sabine asks.

"Well, only if you count the fresh off the truck loaves at the store."

Sabine laughs and says, "Young man, I mean fresh out of the oven?"

"Sabine? Where are my parents?"

"Come on, get yourself something to eat, Therese," Sabine motions to Tre to follow.

"You're stalling. Where are they? I want to get this over with."

When Sabine turns around to face Tre, she steps toward the center of the foyer. Sabine looks down at Tre as she bends and leans, trying not to be seen as the little girl Sabine knew a long time ago.

"I'd rather see my mother than my father. Maybe she can make this fall less painful. Have either of them mentioned me since I left? Maybe say my name? "

"I'm afraid you're not going to see either of them."

"Give me a guess. They already heard I was on the island, didn't they? Wow, this place hasn't changed a bit."

Tre rests her knee on the cushion of a chair against the wall and peers around the corner, as if she and Finkle were playing a bad game of hide and seek as children. Tre was always the one hiding in the hallway closet, taking the same small spot. But she was never able to stay. She'd sneak out to see where Finkle was, and she'd find him tiptoeing around the resting room, looking everywhere. She had no idea he could see her in the large mirror above the fireplace. He watched as she covered her mouth after a giggle escapes her lips, and he pretended he didn't hear anything as she runs back to the closet to hide.

"No, because they are dead."

Whipping around, Tre smiles. She didn't hear that. She must have misheard Sabine. Shaking her head, she snickers and looks back at her. Nervous, Sabine twiddles her fingers and slightly rocks back and forth while standing, staring at Tre. The smile on Tre's face falls.

"Twelve years ago, your mother fell ill. It was pneumonia. The doctors did all they could. But she refused to go to the mainland at your father's request. She was bedridden for about a week before she passed away in her sleep. I never left her side."

Tre collapses onto the cushion as if someone reared their back with all their might and repeatedly punched her in the gut. She is wide-eyed as she looks at Sabine, like a deer caught in headlights. Sabine stands with her hands cupped.

She's calmly smiling, trying to hide the fact she's still hurting as well.

"Your father never remarried per the counsel's request."

The council, ah, the council. It is a group of men who have come together to make difficult and complex decisions for the youth of the island. They act as extra fathers, grandfathers, and uncles, and they occasionally fall in love with those with whom they have a connection. Tre's father was once a member of the council. His children and wife respected, feared, and, above all, misunderstood him. His harshness was sometimes confused with love and compassion. Tre and he clashed when she reached the legal drinking age.

"He loved your mother too much. So, they agreed, and then he lived his life out here. Barely leaving unless he was called. I found him cold, and stiff one morning. He had a heart attack. Doctors said it was instant and he never experienced any pain. I wanted to tell you about your mother, but I was instructed not to."

Tre shakes her head, knowing it's true. If Sabine had tried to contact her, the island's laws would have impaled her on a stake and watched her blood drip, or she would have been banished from her own family.

"How about some freshly sliced bread? I know you have to be hungry after walking all the way here." Sabine says with a smile.

Tre musters a smile from the bottom of her soul and just barely gets the words out, "Sounds great. I'll be right there."

"Good. Good. It's so nice to have you home, Therese. Hurry up before it gets cold or falls."

Tre's smile fades as Sabine turns her back. Tre stares down at the ground, listening to the grandfather clock in the resting room echo through her ears. Her parents are dead, and no one told her, all because she made a choice that was best for her.

CHAPTER 6
HOME SWEET HOME, TRE

AS THE LARGE knife's teeth slash through the fresh loaf of bread sitting on a wooden cutting board, Sabine's veins weave and dive through her dry and wrinkled skin. Tre looks on as golden-brown crumbs fall from the buttered top and land in the steamy and warm center. The bread is fluffy and white, and each slice springs in and out, indicating a rich and sweet flavor.

She remembers the night before she left.

———

Cass, Tre's mother cries as she sits in the resting room. As she listens to Tre and her husband, Jacob scream at each other, she dabs her eyes with a tissue attached to her wrist by a rubber band.

"You have no choice," Jacob says sternly. "I've made my decision."

As Tre takes a step forward, Jacob turns and raises his hand to stop her from speaking any further. Tre comes to a halt, throws her hands up, and collapses on the couch beside Finkle. He feels her frustration and speaks up for her.

"Come on, dad. It's the twenty-second century, not the eighteen hundreds. Things are changing."

"At least it is on the mainland," Tre pipes up.

"We're not on the mainland. We are Islanders with our own set of rules and regulations. Things are never going to change."

"Perhaps it will."

All three of them turned to face Cass, surprised. Tre's eyes widen, Finkle smirks, and Jacob looks at Tre slowly. He backs down. Nobody is supposed to oppose Jacob, the matriarch of the family, the leader, or the family's strong hand. Especially when he is one of the council's strong hands and the next in line to be Mayor when one breathes in death, a nicer way to say "die" on the island.

"I was never given the opportunity to choose my own path. Perhaps we can break the cycle and do the right thing for our daughter. Allow her to grow into something other than a wife and mother. I believe she should be set free. Allow her to travel to the mainland."

Smiling, Tre walks toward Cass to hug and thank her for being on her side for the first time. Well, the first time she had ever heard it. Finkle twists and cracks his neck bones, and falls back into the chair he was in across from Cass. He winks at her as he puts his feet on the small table between them. He's proud of her. Jacob snaps his arm out, stopping her before she reaches Cass. Finkle tilts his head.

"Not going to happen. You will marry and be a mother whether you like it or not. Whether any of us like it. There is a debt and a promise that was made a long time ago. And it must be paid. Simultaneously."

"This is ridiculous," Tre shouted.

As Tre stomps off, Finkle stands, dusts his hands off and stares at his father. "You can forget about those grandkids you've been dreaming about." He bends down and kisses Joseline on the cheek.. "I'm sorry mom."

She pats him on the arm before Finkle walks out, and then Cass looks at her husband as Finkle stomps upstairs. Alone, she looks at Jacob. In disappointment, he shakes his head and leans against the fireplace. He listens to the popping and crackling as the flames flicker their reflection in his eyes.

"Jacob. We can be the change our children need. We owe it to them because of what they did. It's not fair."

"Cass, I love you. But what you say is blasphemy. And what is fair anyway?" Jacob says, never looking at her, but still in the crackling fire.

———

On the stove, a black kettle whistles. Tre returns to reality, realizing she is not alone as she watches Ollie's smile grow big and bright. Ollie's nose tingles as Sabine arranges two large slices on a plate, with a small glass container filled with apricot, strawberry, and orange marmalade jam in the center. As taught by Mrs. Finkle as a child, she always places several options of jam and origami napkins in the morning.

Tre stops Ollie in his tracks with her hand on his arm, and shakes her head.

Sabine huffs and puffs as she carries the platter to the table, saying, "Listen to her. It makes no difference how old I am. My joints creak and moan."

Sabine pulls her apron up to her brow to wipe away sweat as she looks at Ollie, and then back at the platter of delicious bread.

"Well, don't just sit there. You're insulting me if you don't dig in. Mr. Ollie, enjoy."

Taking her advice, Ollie picks a slice of bread up and places a glop of the chunky apricot jam on top. He takes a hearty bite, half the bread, and savors the deliciousness dancing in his mouth.

"Tea?"

Inhaling the rest of the slice, Ollie replies through the chews, "Yes, please."

"Two sugars, I take it."

Ollie shakes his head. Sabine pours tea and drops two cubes of sugar and a squeeze of lemon.

"The lemon gives it a little kick and makes the jam last a little longer on the tastebuds. Theresa, tea?"

Tre dismisses her with a wave. Sabine scoffs. Tre never looks up from the lightly embroidered tablecloth. She traces every stitch and dent with her eyes. Sabine will make sure she has something to drink, no matter what. She walks to the cabinet between the refrigerator and the wall frame. Sabine disappears for a second, retrieves a bottle of scotch, and returns. She arranges it in front of Tre.

"If tea isn't going to solve this..." Sabine taps her fingers against the glass bottle's side. "You will feel a lot better. At least for the night."

"Why didn't anyone tell me?"

Sabine touches Tre's hands, and says, "You know why."

Tre looks up and says, "But she…where are they buried?"

Sabine stands and tries to walk away.

"Sabine."

"It doesn't matter. But I do have something for you."

She walks over to the same cabinet where the scotch is from, bends down, and retrieves a box. She drops it in front of Tre. Dark cherry, with a broken lock in the front hanging off the wood. Sabine opens the box, reaches in, and pulls out a stack of envelopes wrapped in a single red, lacy ribbon.

"Your father would intercept every letter you wrote to your mother. I saw what he was doing by throwing them in the trash and picking them out. Once a week I made sure I got them before the truck came."

"You kept them?"

"Every one of them. I also made sure your mother got them. I would give them to her when it was late at night. Our tea by the fire time. She never said a word when she took it out of my hand. I would finish my cup and go upstairs for a good night's rest. But by the time I woke up, it was just another day to check the trash."

"They don't look open."

"Well. I don't know about that, or why she didn't read them. I think it was the fact you sent them made me feel better. Knowing you were all right. There's more upstairs," Sabine says, teary-eyed.

Tre grabs Sabine's shaking hands together and squeezes them, both holding back tears, especially with Ollie slurping down another cup of tea to push down the bread. Sabine taps Tre's hand and gets up.

"No use reliving the past years and making you sad about something that can never be changed."

"I know," Tre says, playing with the edge of the red ribbon.

As Sabine gathers the platters up, she looks over at Tre and says, "Your brother came by earlier this morning."

Taken aback, Tre blinks a few times. The last time they saw each other, Finkle and her didn't part ways on good terms. Sabine points to the refrigerator.

"He made sure I got all your favorites. Go ahead and look. It's all there. Also, he left you a present upstairs in the guest room to the right."

"The blue room?"

"Yes…the blue room. You remember."

"How can I forget it," Tre says as she looks up.

———

Tre assists Sabine with her coat as Ollie enters the foyer, shoveling another piece of bread smothered in strawberry jam into his mouth. A blob falls to the wood floor. Sabine sees the spread of the red seeding jam falling into the cracks. She lets out a sigh. Fluffing her coat, she watches Ollie lick his fingers for the extra goodness.

"He's a healthy boy."

"He's not a boy, Sabine."

"Well, he acts as if he has never had homemade anything."

Tre leans closer and whispers, "Sometimes a quick meal like fast food or a tv dinner is easier than sweating away at a stove."

"But that's the best part. Sweat, love, and food. It makes it worthwhile when someone like him—" Sabine points and continues, "—devours it. Well, I will see you bright and early in the morning."

Sabine walks to the front door and Tre stops her.

"You don't live here anymore?"

"Baby girl, I haven't lived here in a long time. I have a family. I have grandchildren to cook for. I come back here because I want to, not because I'm needed."

"That doesn't make any sense. Why not just spend time with your family?"

"Easy. You were my family before I had a family."

Tre notices a man in overalls with a pitchfork in the distance. He is staring at her. He wants to be seen. He is dirty like his clothes, and doesn't have an undershirt. Sabine follows Tre's vision line and laughs.

"Don't mind Walter. He's always looking like a statue. He thinks he's scary, but he's nothing more than a smelly old man."

"That he is."

Sabine waves as she leaves and reminds Tre, "Don't forget about the gift your brother left in the blue room."

"Blue room. Got it."

"I'll be back in the morning. Welcome home, Theresa."

"Thanks, Sabine."

Tre takes a cautious step back as Sabine walks down the dirt path, keeping an eye on Walter. He steps back into the pine trees and disappears as she closes the door. Inside, Ollie walks up to her.

"That was the best bread I have ever had," Ollie says.

"Oh, hi Ollie. Nice to see you. No, wait. Hear you. I completely forgot you were here."

"Okay, okay. I know. But I couldn't get enough. It was better than the vending machines. It's like it had a spell over me. I heard nothing, saw nothing except the bread."

"Spell?"

"Yeah, it was like I heard a chorus, or mu…sic," Ollie slows as he notices her look.

Tre scrunches her nose in puzzlement as she throws her duffle bag over her shoulder for the last time in who-knows-how-many years, and slowly ascends the stairs. Various-sized squares, oblongs, and diamond shapes outline the frames that used to be there. A clean and bright space now sits among the rest of the family's photos. Finkle, Cass, and Jacob's pictures are the only ones. She comes to a halt and examines a photograph of her parents, who are smiling on the porch, and Finkle, on the top stairs, the black blob next to him. Tre. After shaking her head, she continues up the stairs as Ollie comes up with an excuse for being "wacko" earlier.

"You can take the Blue Room," she says as she passes, motioning Ollie to it.

"Wow. It's really dark," he shouts.

"Not as dark as mine," she says to herself.

As she passes an annoyingly bright room, Tre steps backward after she notices a white tarp laying in the middle of the room. There were a few humps underneath the tarp. Interested, she steps in. This must be the present Sabine told her Finkle had left for her. On the top is a simple square note which read, "Just a little something from my stash." Crumpling it in hand, she tosses and with one fluid motion, bends down, grabs the tarp, and pulls it.

AA and AAA batteries are stacked in the middle of a sea of black and hunter-green lanterns. The lanterns hug a medium size carnosine lantern heater. Long stemmed candles in multiple colors and candle holders sit next to a smiley face made of match boxes. One of the eyes forms a wink.

"You gotta be kidding me. He has lost it."

She drops the tarp from her hand and walks out. The floor creaks with each step she takes.

She stops at the end of the long, shadowy hallway, staring at a door with tape marks. She hovers her finger over the marks, then closes her fist and she purses her lips. Trying the handle, she is surprised because it's locked. Jingling the handle, she reaches up, over the door's frame, and feels around. A key is lodged between the crack of the frame and the wall. With the tips of her fingers, Tre gets the key and unlocks the door. It's dark.

But not dark like when your eyes are closed, and you fall fast asleep in a wonderful dreamland. .It's not as dark as the corners of a savage's mind wandering in and out of madness, searching for a slit of skin to gnaw and chew on for a while before the next animal crosses their path. And it's not as dark as the resentment Tre had for years toward her parents, especially her father, for always keeping his thumb on her and her mother. Tre has always had nightmares.

She taps the wall, finds the light switch, and flips it on. Nothing happens. Her father must have wanted to keep her hidden, strike her from the family, or erase her, because her room is the only one without power. She is more mature, but somehow, she knew he would be childish and petty about her leaving. With a thud, she drops her duffle, unzips it, and after she digs around, she clicks on a flashlight. She shines it around the room as she slowly walks around.

The blue chair still sits against the pink wall she fought not to have painted. Of course, she lost. Her parents have always wanted her to be their little girl. A happy little girl, and she was. The room is dust and spiderweb friendly, and her favorite gray and black sweater is still folded and lying on the seat.

Her closet is open. Clothes hang from white hangers in the darkness, alone and cold. Plain, solid colors, nothing like the Rolling Stones, AC/DC, and other bands, were never allowed. That never stopped her. She reaches inside and slides out a round hat box. She drags her hand across it, removing the dust and grime. The lid hits the floor as she fights against the suction. She pulls out a black Nirvana shirt she found one day floating on the surface of the mouth when she was fourteen. Cracking a smile, she drops it back inside, remembering walking in the house, soaked head to toe, and telling her parents she "fell" in the water.

Nothing decorates the wall around her, it is barren and boring. Tre was never allowed to have posters or magazine cutouts, despite the fact that teen hipster magazines were all the rage, and every girl had the pages plastered all over her walls and mirrors. Television was another thing Tre was never allowed to watch. They were not appropriate forms of entertainment for the Islanders, or more specifically, the adult Islanders. Why watch something that could seep into their children's minds and tear them away from the way they were meant to live? It wasn't all bad. However, knowing the Top 40 or headbanging songs might have been a welcome change.

Her vanity appears to have been ransacked, despite being as clean as a whistle. She takes out the few empty drawers. Her super-secret diary about her dreams, touching herself, and longing to leave was undoubtedly discovered after she left. She can't imagine what her parents would think when they read it, if they did.

She furrows her brow as she approaches the window, which is the focal point of her room. It's been boarded up. Nail lines run down the sides and burrow in at the top. To let the light back in, she'll need a crowbar.

Swinging her flashlight around, she discovers her twin bed is still military-style. It has perfect tucks at the ends, a triangle down, a pillow perfectly in place, and daisies like it always had when she was ready for bed.

One thing she didn't expect was a stack of letters, wrapped in a single red ribbon with shredded edges, sitting in the middle of her bed. Those must be extra the letters Sabine mentioned downstairs Tre stares and walks over. Examining them in her hands, she confirms that they are the letters she sent to her mother, the ones Sabine placed on the kitchen table. Suddenly, Ollie screams. a long, deep, gut-wrenching scream.

"Ollie!" Tre hollers.

Without hesitation, Tre drops the letters and rushes out, leaving her flashlight behind her. Her steps are loud and rattle the wood, causing the flashlight to bounce on the bed. In the closet, the hat box begins to slide back inside the closet as her hanging clothes move back and forth. Huffing out hard breaths is rare and difficult. Then a long train on the track sighs as the clothes slow and stop as the flashlight rolls inside and then dies out.

Stopping herself as she grabs the door's frame, Tre looks inside the blue room. She starts laughing. Ollie stands on an old wooden chair, scared like a little girl. He is looking down at a black tarantula slowly making its way toward him on the floor. Tre leans forward and folds her arms, watching while still laughing.

"Sheriff, can you do something about that?"

"It's just a spider."

"It's just not a spider. It has venom."

"Sorry to burst your bubble, but tarantula's mouths are too small to even bite you, let alone send venom through your delicate girly veins," Tre says.

She approaches the tarantula and picks it up. It crawls

inside her fingers, over them, and between them. Ollie gets down, stretches his neck, and straightens up his clothes. He's trying to show Tre that he's not as scared or as girly as she claims. Tre grins and begins to walk away.

"Dinner is in the fridge if you want anything."

"I'm good." Ollie touches his stomach, "Actually, I think I ate too much."

Covering his mouth, Ollie hopes he can make it to the adjacent bathroom. The awful sounds of him puking hit the toilet. He leans, slams the door, and continues to get ill. Tre returns to her room and flips on the light switch, which illuminates the room. She comes to a halt. After looking around and seeing everything is in order, she also notices the letters are no longer on the bed. But her attention is turned away when her gaze settles on the tan sheet covering the mirror attached to her vanity. She approaches and is about to pull it off, but stops when she holds the corner of pumpkin colored sheet. There isn't a mirror. She can't recall ever owning or using a mirror as a child. It was always a piece of glass from broken glass, or a windowpane stained with colors made from fallen leaves.

For a moment, the sheriff within Tre calls out to her and yells, "Something is wrong," and she knows it even before the switch fails. She looks around. The room is quiet and serene. Something isn't quite right. But her emotional side yanks at her giving her dizziness, the urge to cry, scream like a banshee, and wail because she had lost the two people she thought were vampires, all-knowing and all-loving to some extent, especially Jacob. It's hard to believe they are no longer alive. She slides her body back out and off the door's frame, listening to her emotional side. As the tarantula walks up her arm, she turns and walks out.

CHAPTER 7
TWO FINKLES AND A GUN

HALF of her body hangs onto the cold wooden floor, while the rest of her body is on a still-made-up bed from the first time she walked into the room. Her snore is small and gradually gets louder as she breathes through her mouth, blowing a string of her hair up and down and sneaking in between her chapped lips. Across the room, the floor creaks as if someone is trying to lightly step on it and not wake her. Like a beacon, Tre's eyes pop open. She counts the steps as they get closer to her, even though she is unable to see who is taking them. She slides her hand under her pillow, and as the footsteps grow closer, her eyes widen. The footsteps stop. Silence. Knowing she's not alone, she listens and tries to adjust her eyes to the dark, hoping to see something—whatever the figure is.

Starting at the end of the bed, she can feel two indents crawling up the mattress. She spins around and flings her arm into the air without hesitation. The movement on the bed comes to a halt. A click is heard. The LED light is very bright. Finkle comes to a halt, nervous and amused, and stares down the barrel of Tre's police-issued gun. He smiles, his gaze shifting back and forth between her and the barrel.

"Morning sis."

Tre cocks her weapon.

"Wanna go for a run?" Finkle asks.

The click makes Finkle nervous, and he swallows loudly enough for both to hear. Tre's stare was unwavering as she tilts her head, as if the game they're playing has just become more interesting, especially now that she has the upper hand.

"Coffee sounds better," he looks at the weapon, "and new underwear too."

Finkle slides back off the bed, and Tre watches, still following him with her weapon. He smiles at her as if he is daring her to shoot. She even considers it for a second. But, of course, her bark is louder than her bite. In one swift move, Finkle yanks the blinds open. Tre shields herself like a vampire as the sun shines in her eyes, blinding her and causing a headache.

"I think you might need these."

Finkle pulls two magazines for Tre's gun from his back pockets, tossing them on the bed. She looks at the bottom of her gun and sees that the magazine is missing. Tre places her weapon on the bed's end table and collapses back onto the bed. Finkle chuckles and places them on the end table. He swings the lantern back and forth in his fingers, enjoying seeing Tre in pain. He turns his head and inhales.

"I smell bacon."

Tre moans and mumbles something that Finkle can't make out. He cups his hand to his ear.

Tre mumbles, "I hate you so much."

"I'm sorry, what was that?"

"I said," Tre stands up quickly, her head spinning.

The room blinds her as she covers her eyes and tries to hold her head on her shoulders as it spins. She almost pukes. Finkle chuckles as he strikes the door frame with the edge of his boot and hollers on purpose, ensuring that his voice carries at her.

"Better get a move on or you're going to be late for your

first day on the job. Back on little ole Pine Island," Finkle says in a loud Southern Louisiana accent.

Tre drops back onto the bed and places her pillow over her head. She screams. She holds the pillow in place, and quickly regretting it. That was a bad idea as the pain radiated causing her to smother her whimper.

Sizzling bacon bounces off every corner of the kitchen; it's the best smell. Eggs sit in a brown woven basket waiting for their turn in the hot sauna of the cast-iron skillet, and steam from the biscuits flows through the air as they are set in the middle of the table. Fresh orange juice sits bubbling with no seeds in a glass-rimmed pitcher.

Sabine turns the eggs sunny side up and pours three circles into a skillet. Finkle enters and places the lantern on the counter. Sabine turns to face him, threateningly pointing her skillet flipper at him.

"Don't even think about leaving that hunk of junk on my counter. On the floor in the other room," Sabine tells Finkle, motioning out the door.

"Your counter?" Finkle teases as he grabs her, dips her, and then steals a couple of strips of bacon.

"Boy, out. Get over there and do something. Like, get…"

She rolls her eyes as Finkle pops her back up and walks around her. She is more familiar with Finkle than he is.

He jumps onto the counter and eats bacon like a child who loves bucking semi-authority figures, even if they have been with the family or like family for his whole life. Tre walks in, as if death had triumphed over sleep. Breaking a piece of bacon in two, Finkle stops as Tre walks in. Disheveled, tired, and drunk, Finkle examines her.

"What? No gun?" Finkle asks.

Sabine turns around holding a plate full of eggs, and says, "Gun?"

Her eyes dart back and forth between Finkle and Tre. "There better not be guns in this house."

"I'm a cop, Sabine."

"I know, I know. Still, it better be in its little wallet and not flinging around this house."

"It's called a holster," Tre replies as she shields her eyes from the brightness of the sun's rays beaming inside around them.

"It's called a holster, Sabine," Finkle leans in still on the counter, informing Sabine as if she didn't hear Tre the first time.

"Please tell me you two are not at it again."

"He started it," Tre states as she walks over and begins pouring herself a cup of coffee.

"He started it," Finkle mocks as he hops down.

He grabs the lantern, sitting it down beside him as he sits at the table. He flips the edge of Tre's wild hair. She swings at him, misses him by a few inches, and laughs as he heads to the table.

"Man, your aim sucks."

"Man, your aim sucks," Finkle mocks in a high-pitched voice.

"Real mature, Jacob," Tre says.

"Come on get yourself some breakfast. Before it gets cold," Sabine says, pushing Tre to the table.

"Looks like someone was having a drink without me," Finkle says.

He smirks as he piles his plate with biscuits, more bacon, and scrambled eggs. He looks at Tre, who has her head down and is staring at the black coffee she is trying to nurse while rubbing her temples. Tre is already annoyed by the boisterous tone in Finkle's voice.

"What are you talking about?"

"The mess you made in the dining room last night. And the mess Sabine cleaned up."

He points with his fork to the dining room. Tre leans back to avoid the egg pieces as she looks toward the dining room. It's hard to see inside at the angle she is sitting in the kitchen. The large black stove is blocking her vision, so she leans further back.

With his mouth full and pieces of egg shooting out, Finkle says, "You're lucky she never cut herself."

Flopping back in her chair, Tre tries to remember what happened last night. She doesn't remember a thing. She narrows her eyes and looks around, completely confused. Sabine steps in front of Tre, smiling and holding a vintage aluminum six-inch coffee pot. Curling her wrist, Sabine tries to hide the white gauze wrapped around her hand.

"What happened to your hand?"

Sabine smiles and begins to pour more coffee for Tre. "Nothing."

"Nothing my ass. She cut herself from the shattered glass you caused."

"I didn't–all I did was put a spider outside last night. Then I went to bed."

"Is that what they call getting drunk on the mainland? Putting the spider out." Finkle laughs as he shoves the rest of his eggs in his mouth .

"Oh, it's all right, Miss Tre."

"You're too nice, Sabine." Finkle tells her as he heads out of the kitchen.

Tre leaps from her chair and follows Finkle. Sabine closes her eyes, not caring if she will be able to stop the war that is about to break out in the Finkle household. She turns and walks behind Tre. As Tre appears around the corner, Finkle opens the front door.

"Hey. Hey. You got a problem with me?"

Finkle turns and stares at her. "Yeah, I do."

"Why? I haven't been here for twenty-four hours, and you've had a piss poor attitude."

He closes the door, "I have a bad attitude! You walk back on this island thinking you know more than anyone and expect people to listen to you."

"The hell are you talking about? I am here for a job, and then I'm outta here."

"Then do it. It's better you leave as fast as you can. Because…"

Finkle stops when he sees Sabine peering around the corner, staring and listening. Tre folds her arms and waits. She wants the real answer, not the one he wants her or Sabine to hear. But the truth is that he has always had a problem with telling the truth.

"Because you are already causing problems."

Finkle yanks the door open and stomps down the porch's steps. Tre walks out. Forget the headache, she has a pain in the ass, and his name is Finkle.

"Like what? From what I see, this place has a lot of problems…"

Finkle stops and rolls his eyes. His breathing quickens, and he rushes up to Tre, looking her in the eyes. His pupils dilate and fill with rage. He tries to remain silent. He clenches his fist, frustrated that she can't see how her presence has changed the air around them, the residents' attitudes, and the house they're standing in. Everything has changed, and Tre is the only one who isn't feeling it like a shiver down the spine, a fire ant's sting, or the sting of a scorpion's tail.

"How about you hurry up and do what you do Sheriff. For me, Sabine, Barney Fife upstairs, and for yourself. Before it's too late."

"What's that supposed to mean? she asks as she flings her arms in the air.

"Oh my god, you are so dense," Finkle yells as he turns in a circle back to the front door.

"What's with the yelling?"

In his uniform, Ollie stands in the middle of the stairs, looking down. He doesn't look good. He looks like someone beat him with an ugly stick, as the old saying goes. His skin is pale, not sheet pale but with a hue of blue, and his lips are thinning. Finkle and Tre stare at him.

"Did I miss breakfast?"

"It's on the table. Let me make you some fresh oatmeal and eggs," Sabine replies.

Ollie rushes down the steps like a chicken with its head cutoff. Sabine wraps her arms around Ollie's shoulders and ushers him into the kitchen.

"Is that fresh orange juice?"

"Why yes, it is. Someone has a nose for menus, don't they." Sabine laughs.

Tre turns back to Finkle as he is already down the steps and walking away.

"Why do you hate me so much?" She hollers after him.

"Use your copper skills, then get back to me."

"Same old Finkle. You haven't changed a bit have you," Tre yells.

Finkle turns halfway down the dirt road and flips her off. Unsurprisingly, she flips him off with both hands. As Finkle disappears down the path and into the woods, they continue to raise their middle fingers higher and higher. Sabine shakes her head in the doorway.

"I see he hasn't changed," Tre says.

"He has. You just haven't been around to see it."

"You're always on his side. Just like when we were kids."

"I am not. I am on both of your sides because I see them both. And you both can be assholes."

Tre's eyes widen in shock.

"What? I can cuss. I just don't think it's lady-like at times."

Tre laughs as she walks inside and towards the stairs." I am loving this Sabine." She moves her hand up and down like

Vanna White showing off blank squares. "She's different from what I remember. I hope she stays. Maybe she can help with that asshole brother of mine."

"I'm so happy the kids are getting along."

A knock breaks up their conversation. A Junior Marshall is standing in the open doorway. He has wide shoulders like a Marine, and he looks at Sabine while sucking in his little gut.

"Sorry the door was open. Y'all didn't hear me." He clears his throat. "Sabine, good morning. Marshall Spence has asked Deputy Boden to accompany him as he does a walk on the Mouth's edge."

"Jamieson does that?" Sabine inquires as Tre takes a few steps up.

The Junior Marshall scowls and replies to Sabine for Tre. "He doesn't want any mainlanders crossing over without and ruining our happy community."

"Yeah, happy."

Tre walks up the stairs and around the corner, leaving the Junior Marshall alone and staring.

CHAPTER 8
HER NAME IS THE
WOMAN IN THE WOODS

BLACK TREES COVER a large portion of the roadside. With each pull of the bird's curved beak and its rhythmic rise and fall like waves in the tide, the sickening chokes become harsher.

Small, muddy, maggot-infested pieces of rigged meat hang out of its mouth and slosh around as it goes back for another bite. The red-rimmed head, wart-strewn neck, and three-times-larger chin emit an uncontrollable hunger.

A white, swollen muscle brushes against its beak as it tears at the bone, hungry for more moist food. When boot heels hit the black pavement near the curve, whistles can be heard. Finkle comes to a complete stop and crushes the loose gravel, which is unusual for the island. Three condors turn their heads toward him, looking under their wet, leathery-like feathers.

They step in front of the roadkill they have been feasting on for a morning delight. Their eyes are dark and empty, yet ravenous. One of the condors, the biggest, slowly chews and looks at Finkle with delight. They hope he will be the next flesh they devour as an afternoon snack or a midnight breakfast.

Finkle doesn't have time to react to the condors as an

arrow appears from the woods and embeds itself inside a tree across from the condor. The condor takes flight. Their wing-span is five centimeters long, from one to the other. The wickedness of the old, wrinkled bodies begins to soar into the sky and hide in the treetops. The hunter emerges. The hunter looks up as he approaches the arrow, inspecting the few feathers it has gathered. He then approaches the roadkill. All Finkle can do is watch in astonishment.

———

The Hunter bends downward. He can't make out what animal it is. But it doesn't matter. He yanks a laundry sack from his side and scoops it up. No gloves, no shovel—not even with his shoe—but with his bare hands. Finkle grabs his stomach as he watches the guts ooze with creamy pink and charred colors as it flops inside the bag with a plop. The smell is horrible, rotten, and puke worthy. Finkle covers his mouth and nose to save himself from it, but it's too late. He can't.

Fingertips wrap around the raccoon's tail as the hunter pulls it from the pavement. It's sticky, and the wild hairs cry as it unlatches. The hunter holds it up like a trophy. Too bad no one snapped a picture for the mantel. Smiling, his teeth are chipped, while the ones that are missing are filled with black-ened gums and a sliced tongue.

"Momma is going to be proud of me."

He laughs. Then he sinks his chipped teeth into the raccoon's buttocks and rips a medium-sized bite. As he chews the meat like gum, maggots fall from the edge of his mouth and onto the pavement. He turns to Finkle to see his reaction. Finkle hunches over, coughing, trying not to let the vomit tickling his throat come up. He gives the hunter a thumbs up without looking.

Finkle turns away and listens as the hunter takes another bite. Finkle makes his way to the end of the tree line. He braces his hand against the tree, hoping the hunter will hurry and leave. Eyes closed, Finkle waits for the nausea to pass and the smell to dissipate. When he opens his eyes, that's when he sees the small, lacy edge of a piece of fabric, dirty and wet. The lace forms a line that leads into the woods. The dark woods. Finkle fears what's inside. He turns to leave when he hears a weak whimper. Through the darkness, faint and in the distance. He steps back as the shadow roams closer. He refuses to go inside. He turns to walk away, but another whimper stops him. This time, he can't ignore the words.

"Help." In the distance, a faint female whimper.

"I'll get you, someone," he yells to her from the side of the road.

"Help me."

Because he forgot his lantern at his parent's house, he checks his pockets, thinking he could have a small flashlight. He doesn't. He has to do something. He turns back.

"Fuck."

He takes a few deep breaths to relax and looks up at the sky, as the sun only illuminates specific parts of the wooded area. He makes sure to keep in the light, never touching the dark. He pushes a tree limb back, stopping before it disappears into the darkness. He steps into a puddle of water, he tries to get out, but he can't. Not wanting it to stay any longer than he has to, he pulls his feet out of his boots quickly. With his body and steps, he draws a path in the sunlight like someone threw a bag of rice onto a canvas and is tracing it with a black marker.

The whimper grows louder as he makes his way to the middle of a small opening. He knows this opening because it is where he and Tre played as children, inside and around the town, with large trees. Criss-crossed and circled like a game of Xs and Os, Finkle moves his way around as he listens to the whimpering female. Dodging and bending around trees, he finally sees a woman lying against a trunk. The bottom of her white, lacy dress with bundles of cherries on it is slashed, and her brown hair drapes along the jagged edges. Her skin is peach and red.

"It's going to be all right."

The sunlight beams downward in bigger spots, which makes it easier for him to quicken his pace. He finally makes his way to the moaning and whimpering female by climbing over a sunny portion of the surrounding trunks. At last, he will leap, and he will be able to comfort her and see her injuries before getting help.

But he freezes as his heart rate rises above normal. He sways to the left. He vomits. He flees, long, gooey, slime-like spit trailing from his lips. The whimpering woman is no longer alive. Her eyes are wide open and coated with white soap, which has dulled and turned her green eyes ghostly. Bright red and dark red blood splatters resemble freckles on her face. What's left of her feet have baby pink polish where her toes would have been. On one of her hands, all fingernails have fallen off. Looking around, Finkle finds they are attached to the lacy section of her dress, like staples. A large chunk of succulent, swollen flesh rests in her other hand, still raw in her throat, but claw and tooth marks surround it. Inside her throat, there is no muscle or blood inside her esophagus, and it is smooth and clean.

Flies circle the body of the woman as Ollie moves in closer for a better shot with his camera. Mushy and wet, Ollie steps into a mixture of pine, dirt, and broken bark, along with large noodles and clumps; her intestines. He lifts his foot, stares at the bottom of his boot, and thinks, *I wonder what Sabine is making for dinner.* Maybe biscuits and gravy. His mouth waters the longer he stares. The redness and gravy-style guts make his stomach growl. Snapping back to reality, he continues to take pictures. Hesitating, he sees the dried blood on her lips reminding him of spaghetti sauce. He would give anything to taste her last meal. Tre's loud voice distracts him.

"So, you're saying she ripped out her own throat?"

Tre stands watching Marshall Spence and one of his deputies talk, and confident that every word coming out of their mouths is factual and true. Marshall Spence smirks as he folds his arms. Tre motions back toward the female as Ollie walks slowly around the body, examining and noting her .

"How about the dress's hem, lined with her fingernails?"

Marshall Spence doesn't have to say anything as his deputy, a mini-him, walks towards the body. He nudges Ollie back as he prepares to snip one of the fingernails off and slip it into the small plastic bag.

"Sounds impossible if you ask me. There is no way right before or as she bled out, the killer was able to stitch them on."

"Actually, that's impossible," Ollie says, clearing his throat.

Ollie does not let the deputy's eye daggers stop him from speaking as he carefully steps around him, never touching him. One, because the deputy will not move, and two, Ollie avoids making enemies. But it's too late.

"One, she would have had to rip her throat out first, which you mentioned. But her nails could or would be embedded in the skin around it, if not broken. They are perfectly intact, and the polish looks fresh," Ollie says as he bends down to inspect the fingernails.

"And what about her feet?" Tre finishes as she turns to Marshall Spence.

A gentle breeze blows through the crime scene and down Tre's silky long black ponytail, carrying a hint of her grape-fruit and mint aroma. Tickling Marshall Spence's nostril and wrapping around the hair inside, he steps back and covers his nose. To him, it smells more like freshly burned ashes. He begins to sweat like melting tar. But he tries to keep his position and his authority.

"She's always had problems with them. The doctor in town will confirm that. No bathing will cause a lot of things, especially since she's been living in the woods since she was in her twenties or so."

Marshall Spence walks off and Tre shouts, "What is her name?"

"The Woman in the Woods."

"You gotta be kidding me. What's her real name, Marshall Spence?"

Marshall Spence stops and turns to her. He has had enough, and he lets her know.

"None of this has anything to do with you, Sheriff Finkle. This isn't your district. So, if you don't mind, I think you need to take your deputy and go stand behind the caution tape with the other residents. And let the professionals take over."

"Professionals? You are telling me she committed suicide. Why? Where's the note?"

"Like I said, professionals. Get moving, Sheriff. Don't forget your little buddy over there."

He winks at her with a click of his tongue. She turns to Ollie, frowning in disgust. A few more deputies form a barrier in front of Ollie's view of the body. He leans forward, seeing a slight opening between two of the deputy's bodies, and they snap it shut. Tre looks around.

Zoning into her surroundings, the voices of everyone around slowly form into disconnected voices. The caution tape flicks separately from left to right. Little bluebirds chirp and then slowly turn into long, drawn-out caws. The residents stare at her, shuffle their feet in the loose leaves as they turn their backs, and she hears the deep sighs they exhale. She looks at

Marshall Spence as he writes on a clipboard with a ballpoint pen. As he finishes, the ink flows evenly and his gaze darts to her like fingernails on a chalkboard. She turns in a circle, looking down all five paths, now covered by fallen trees.

"Where's the note?" She quietly asks herself.

She steps forward toward the body. But the deputies block her view. She pushes through, they hold her, but she can see the body. She makes a mental note that the body is clean despite being mangled. She pushes off the deputies.

"Hey. What's going on?" Marshall Spence yells.

"She's not listening to orders, sir."

"Where's the note?"

"What note?"

Ollie knows exactly what Tre is talking about, and he looks around in the outer areas, near the body. Marshall Spence watches in wonderment. The light isn't as bright as he thinks it is upstairs. Ollie looks at Tre and shakes his head. Tre smiles and turns her attention to Marshall Spence.

"Without a suicide note, I have to take into consideration that she might have been murdered. Possibly by the person or people who kidnapped Colby Morel."

"There's no evidence the Morel boy was kidnapped," Marshall Spence speaks up.

"And there's isn't any to say he wasn't. These two cases might be related, and as the visiting Sheriff on the behalf of the DA, I invoke mainland laws. Which means I have the power until these two cases are solved.

"You can't…"

"Oh yes, I can."

Tre's matter-of-fact voice trails off as she pulls her red pen from her pocket and uses it to show the sewn fingernails on the Woman in the Woods dress's edge.

"See these nails? This is called a French manicure. Now, I know you can't do this here on the island. But on the mainland, you can."

Defeated, Marshall Spence stares at her as the residents of the island turn and look to him for answers. He is speechless. She has him by the balls. He knows mainland laws are here to stay and trump the few they have on the island. Tre smiles. Marshall Spence lets out a loud sigh and lazily waves his hand, letting his deputies know to move. Ollie steps in and continues to take pictures and make notes.

"Now, Marshall," Tre says as she steps toward him. "I'm going to need files dating back five years—no, ten years would be better."

"And why would that be?"

Tre leans in closer and he bends his head down to hear her. She whispers, "Come on, Jamieson. You know why. I need to see what the fuck has been happening on this island. I'll be in your office in ten. Oh, and please make certain that none of your deputy's tamper with my evidence. Because if they do, I'll know."

Marshall Spence snaps his eyes onto Ollie as he bends and curves his body, not touching the Woman in the Woods as he angles his camera to get a good shot of the claw marks on her neck. Then, with her cloudy eyes, Tre walks off in search of Finkle. Marshall Spence calls out to her.

"You might want to speak to the witness who found her. You never know; he could have something to do with it, Sheriff Finkle."

"I know how to do my job, Marshall. Why don't you come with me? You might learn something," Tre hollers as she disappears down the pathway back to the main road.

Tree limbs hang low, parts of the path chilled by the shadows because they never feel the warmth of the sun. Low in the bundle of green leaves and pine straw, a pair of blue eyes follow Tre as she passes. It's a young teenage boy. He pulls out a cell phone. He texts in the group chat. His name is Bear.

BEAR

The Woman in the Woods is dead. The
Sheriff has taken over.

Messages from different animal names flood in.

TIGER

No way!

SQUIRREL

Should we tell?

POLAR

Hell no.

HAWK

I think we should keep watching. No cawing
y'all.

SQUIRREL

But it will come for another.

HAWK

No, Squirrel. We don't know if we can trust
her yet.

TIGER

She's still one of them, no matter how long
she's been gone.

BEAR

I'll take care of it. I know exactly what to do.

Bear flips his phone shut. Then leaves as fast as he can.

Finkle is pacing on the main road when Tre approaches
him.

"It's not surprising that you're being looked at. How are
you doing?"

"Oh, fine, despite the fact I found a woman basically ripped to shreds. Other than that, I'm good. I've never seen anything like that before."

"Yeah, me neither. How about you go home and get some rest. I'll come by in a few hours and take your statement."

"Getting drunk sounds more appealing, besides I need to stop by and tell Rob."

Finkle walks off, and Tre has a puzzled look on her face.

"Wait a minute, tell Rob what? This, like the Motel case, is an ongoing investigation. I would prefer you to just go home."

Finkle looks at her and indicates towards the woods. "That woman. Your case. That's Rob's younger sister. Sadie."

Tre looks around and tries to quickly place the jigsaw pieces. She has no idea that Sadie was never missing, she simply vanished.

"Sadie vanished for no apparent reason nearly three years ago. Only Rob and I were aware she was in the woods. She left our society because she claimed it had called her."

"Who called her?"

"Not who. But what. The thing in the dark. The same thing I have been saying."

"Someone killed her, Finkle. There's nothing in the dark. Not a campfire story or a folktale, a real human like you, like me."

"I hope we never find out. Now I have to tell him that he's the last member of his family on the island."

Tre watches Finkle walk away while listening to crickets sing. It's strange how nocturnal animals are awake during the day and sleep at night.

CHAPTER 9

ONLY TWO BOXES

THE KNOCK on the door is deafening enough to awaken the dead. Sabine pulls it open. Levi is standing in front of her. He has two boxes in his hands. He smiles at Sabine as she holds the door edge in her palm.

"Levi Dowser. You haven't been to the house in a long time."

"I know. Work—well, Marshall Spence—keeps me busy."

"Well. Come on in. Is there anything I can get you? Tea? How about a large, fresh cinnamon roll with cranberry spread, topped with dark brown sugar and lots of love?" Sabine inquires as Levi enters the foyer.

Just thinking about taking a bite and feeling the warmth of the brown sugar and tartness of the cranberries makes Levi's mouth water. But he shakes his head.

"No, thank you, Sabine. But I promise to save it for another day in the rain."

"You save it for that rainy day."

Tre walks from the back of the house, pushing up her sleeves. Levi stares at her like she's Cinderella arriving at the ball. Sabine takes a step back because she doesn't want to interrupt and walks out of the foyer. Tre steps down off the last step with a thud, bringing Levi out of his daydream of a princess and prince.

"I have the files you requested."

"Wow. So, business-like. I'm impressed."

"I don't know what you mean?"

"I don't remember you being so… mature."

"Do you want me to go back out and throw pebbles at your window? Because I can." His smile widens as he observes Tre's shyness, which he has always admired in her as a child. His stupid remarks and actions could easily make her blush, as she is now.

Through her giggles, Tres says, "No. I was just saying you're mature."

"People change, Tre."

Tre nods and looks down at the boxes. Two. She had not expected only two. Is Marshall Spence not sending everything because Tre yanked the dick from his hands and took over stoking, per se, because she demasculinized him in front of her deputies? Or does he have a problem with her because she turned him down when they were teens? Is her past coming back to bite her? Levi's smile is odd, and he's acting shy right now. He quickly switches from lost love to professional. He sets the boxes down on the floor.

"Please tell me this isn't everything?"

"It is."

Tre removes the top box. As her eyes widen, loose pieces of paper fall from her grasp. She probes a little further. To her surprise, the entire box is lacking files. She closes her eyes and presses her hands against the box's lips before turning to face Levi.

"Let me guess. The second box is the same way."

"Worse. Most in there are handwritten and faded."

"Great," Tre exclaims as she closes the top box.

As the electricity charges between them, there is an

awkward silence. Tre stares, waiting for Levi to say something. Levi becomes more nervous and opens his mouth to try to speak. It is humorous because when Levi was younger, he was the talker of the town, the gossiper, and the one teen everyone went to for the dirt. He always had something to say, and he knew how he wanted to be heard. Now, he's silent as a dead sheep, and the big bad wolf stands, rolling her eyes. Just waiting for the right moment to strike, or for her to get to work and go home. Neither has to worry about it any longer; Levi's Marshall radio goes off with a deep, radiating beep and makes him jump.

"Levi?" a male's voice snaps.

"Junior Marshall Dowser here."

"Where are you at?"

"I'm at the Finkle house."

"Still? Why? It should have been an easy drop-and-run. As the Marshall says, we aren't supposed to converse with mainlanders, let alone the enemy."

Tre purses her lips and turns her head, trying to avoid laughing at the stupidity of the guy over the radio and the frame of mind Marshall Spence is planting inside his deputies' pea-sized brains. She is grateful to have gotten away.

"All right, Pete. Is there something you needed?"

"Yeah, Marshall Spence needs you at the Mason homestead. The cows got loose and have trapped Old Man Mason up a tree again."

"Tell him to hang on and I'm on my way."

Levi takes a step toward the door. He returns his attention to Tre as she gathers the boxes in her arms. He swallows and clears his throat.

"I know it's been a while. But if you want. We could meet for a drink at Sadie's. You know, to catch up and all."

Tre thinks for a minute, then says, "Sure."

"Yeah? Yeah. Okay. I'll…"

"Levi, where are you? The cows are getting mad. Now they have a deputy up a tree."

"You better go. I'll catch up with you tomorrow or something like that. If you're not trapped in a tree."

"Levi to the rescue."

"Always."

Levi pauses for a moment before closing the door. He wanted to say something, but he knew his radio was going to go off. They will, however, have their drink date. If there is a date at all.

Pulling another loose sheet of paper out of the box, a blob of mustard drops onto it. Ollie stares at it as he tries to wipe it away, smearing it and blending the penciled words. Most of them vanish. He doesn't dare to take a bite of the roast beef hoagie with his mouth full, so he crumples it and tosses it into the waste can beside him. Tre never sees as she moves closer to the window, into the sunlight, and holds up a piece of paper to the light. She squints her eyes and tries to read it. She even leans in closer, as if it will help. No, it does not.

"It's got to be a bad joke. Who in their right mind writes files in pencil?"

Ollie mumbles, "Don't they have a computer or something?" with another large bite in his mouth.

Tre sighs and shakes her head. "The island isn't what I call tech friendly. They have typewriters and old credit card slide machines, but nothing like we do. It's as if they're still in the 1800s."

Sabine walks in with a tray of steaming tea, three cups resting on blue saucers, and a small container of sugar cubes. The tray also holds a cow-shaped cream dispenser and a small coffin filled with edible flowers and sugar cookies.

"All right. Here we go. Cookies and tea to commemorate the start of The Shredding tomorrow night."

Scarecrow cookies in various shapes and sizes, drenched in red icing with arms out and brown icing strung long like pine straw, as well as bells stitched together in a variety of colors.

"Ooo, cookies. Thanks, Sabine."

Tre turns and watches. Instantly, Ollie hops on them like a child eating vanilla-flavored paste, smashing a roach under a barefoot, or having a tea party with headless dolls. For Tre, it's more like someone dropping dirt on a fresh grave.

"Already that time?" Tre exclaims.

She finishes looking at the paper in her hand. She couldn't read it no matter what, even with the sun shining through the window she was standing by.

"Surely, you remember."

"It's something I prefer to forget."

"You know how we live, Theresa."

Tre turns to Sabine who is staring at her with disappointment. "Nothing personal, Sabine. Just how it is."

"It doesn't feel that way."

"Why?" Ollie asks as he gathers a few cookies in hand and Sabine pours them a cup of tea.

"Why what?" Sabine wonders as she turns to Tre dropping empty manilla folders on the table.

"He wants to know why Islanders live the way they do," Tre answers for Ollie, whose mouth is once again full.

"We are normal. We just prefer the quiet, isolated beauty away from the chaotic, apocalyptic, and mundane world."

"Apocalyptic? Now that's taking it too far. The mainland isn't that bad. I mean look at me," Ollie replies as small pieces of cookie fly out of his mouth and onto the table.

Sabine rakes the crumbs into her hands, places them in her apron, and laughs as Ollie stands, showing himself like a model walking the catwalks. No one wants to watch because the fashion is so nerdy and pitiful. As nice as she is, Sabine finds Ollie interesting.

"Mr. Ollie, you are simply incredible," Sabine compliments as she gives Tre a cup of tea. She turns to the box, where she continues to take out the files for Tre.

"No matter how different our traditions are from yours, we all want the same thing. A family. A family that will continue with what our ancestors started so we can be overall a clean and loving community. Nothing more and nothing less. That's why we prefer to be self-sufficient in every way with no technology, except for the radio our Marshalls use, along with two vehicles. Oh, and the boats, like Jacob's boat to gather fresh seafood, and the towers that run the lights. Gardening, waterholes, etc.…."

"Plus, no outside influence whatsoever besides the earth as their teacher," Tre interrupts. "See, I remember a few things."

Tre can detect the scent of peppermint. She has loved the scent since she was a child. Sabine always gave her small green and white peppermint candies instead of hot cinnamon candies. She would tell her that the color of nature on the island made them healthier. She takes a small sip, smooth and calming. Tre succumbs to the hypnotic taste.

"And…"

"Perfect. I forgot what it tasted like."

"Oh, please. You never forget things. You have a mind like your father. Strong as an ox and placed in tiny compartments for those quiet nights."

Oddly, Sabine mentions Tre's father. Since he was the reason she left. Besides, Finkle was more like him than she was. He was the pride and joy of the family. Reaching for folder a stack of photos slips out and lands at his feet. He picks one up. Ollie gasps.

"What is it?" Tre asks.

Tre takes the picture from Ollie.

"I thought technology wasn't on the island." Tre says.

"It wasn't." Sabine wipes the wrinkle from her apron. "But I do remember something about a camera being found or something like that." She waves Tre off with a grin as she walks across the room. "It was a long time ago, and my mind isn't what it used to be."

Her pupils dilate. At the window, Sabine looks at her reflection with a sly smile and narrow eyes. Before Tre lifts and looks at Sabine her sly smile vanishes, curling up, and reaching ear-to-ear; her eyes widen with joy. Ollie grabs another scarecrow cookie and beheads it with a crunch.

"When did the Dolson twins vanish?"

"Oh, about twelve years ago," Sabine says, turning her back to open the blinds. "It's going to get dark soon."

Tre examines the picture. Moses and Abigail Dolson, fifty years old, stand in the middle of the field, their faces blank, their hands on their mother's shoulders as she sits in the wheelchair she has used since her early twenties. She is the only one who is happy. On the island, there were whispers that they were plagued by nightmares of living trees and whispers that made them giggle and tickle. That, however, is impossible.

"They remind me of the twins from The Shining. What's that thing in the corner of the picture?" Ollie wonders as he takes another bite from the cookie.

A shadow of hands holding ropes in the shape of symbols appears on the right side of the image. They are hazy, and only the Dolson Twins understand what they mean, no one does unless they were taught.

"They were deaf. All of them were."

"The entire family?"

"Strange, I know. But true."

"Let us not speak of the dead. We must remember them as they were. Silent and loved."

Comfortable, Sabine sways back and forth, sharing the

sunset rays with the dining room. She refuses to discuss the Dolson twins or their family. She has never been one to discuss the past, especially those who have lived strange, unusual, and tragic lives. She takes a deep breath and gathers herself. Sabine brings her hands in prayer and thinks as she rubs her index fingers on her bottom lip.

"Now what shall we have for supper? Ollie, I'm sure you have plenty of ideas. I'm thinking chicken with white gravy seasoned with a little thyme and rosemary. Collard greens, freshly husked corn, and for dessert..."

"I wonder how Isaiah feels about being the only one left to carry on his family name. Especially here on the island."

"Banana nut bread topped with pecans and salted caramel."

"Excellent choice, Ollie. Banana nut bread it is."

Sabine walks away. Tre has a piece of paper in each hand. Her gaze darts back and forth. She notices something. Leave it to her if it's just one small piece of a larger puzzle. Whether anyone wants her to or not, she will make it work. Tre slaps Ollie on the back, causing him to nearly choke on the tea he's drinking .

"Let's get to work. It's going to be a long night." Tre leans back and calls out to Sabine, "Keep the tea coming, Sabine."

"And cookies," Ollie hollers.

CHAPTER 10
APPLE CIDER, ANYONE?
IT'S GOOD

THE MIDDAY SUN peaks over the clouds nosey to what is happening on Pine Island. The stack on top of the house is billowing a steady stream of smoke as Tre and Ollie walk down the dirt road toward it. They pass a black mailbox with the name Forgeron painted on the side. Ollie looks around, and his eyes land on a man in overalls hacking away at a large log. Large like Paul Bunyan, with a long black beard and shoulder-length hair, his muscles are intimidating. The man stops mid-hack and stares. Ollie pushes his glasses up his nose and clears his throat. Tre can see his discomfort.

"He looks scarier but is really a teddy bear."

"How do you know?"

"It's just a guess."

"Oh, that's comforting to know.

Three wooden rocking chairs, large and small, are neatly stacked against the side of the house, which has a wrap-around porch. The house itself is not one color, but the green roof stands out.

"Remember, we are here to ask about Katie. Don't mention anything about Colby."

"I still think we need to drill the Morel parents."

"I agree, but they are acting like nothing happened. They

89

are too busy getting ready for the Shredding. It's like Colby's disappearance never happened. Something isn't right. According to the files, the last disappearance was more than fifteen years ago. But Katie disappeared only three years ago."

"How do you know that?"

"A little raven with a badge told me."

Almost to the house, Ollie comes to a halt as the scent of apple cider and cinnamon wafts through the screen from the open front door and teases his nostrils. Ollie takes a long, deep breath. Tre continues, but when she notices he isn't beside her, she turns back. When she turns around, she sees him moving his hands in a circular motion, allowing the aroma to envelop him.

"There's something else we are missing. I can feel it. Try not to drink them out of the house and at home. Be professional."

"I know, I know. I just can't help myself."

Tre turns her head as they ascend the porch steps, "Try."

"Que veux-tu? (What do you want?)"

Tre and Ollie stop on the porch's edge, their feet barely on the steps as they look toward the screen door, where Mr. Forgeron stands. His arms crossed, he stares them down like a guard dog, daring intruders to enter his palace. His face stubble, like his hair, is salt and pepper; his laid-back yellow and black shirt is too small as if it shrank in the dryer, and his jeans are patches of dark blue fabric. He casts a glance past where Tre stands, toward Ollie.

"Mr. Forgeron, we are here to discuss Katie. Your step-daughter."

He hears nothing and sternly asks again, "Que veux-tu? (What do you want?)"

Tre shakes her head and nudges Ollie.

"Uh-uh-Mr. Forgeron, we—I—we—I—we are here to discuss Katie."

As his sternness fades, a smile appears, and his eyes sparkle. His hand strikes the screen, pushing it open, and he welcomes Ollie inside with open arms.

"Please come in, Deputy. We're delighted to have you in our presence."

Ollie steps forward, constantly turning his head back and forth from Tre to Mr. Forgeron. Tre motions him to go inside as the screen door slams shut in her face with a loud bang. She is not welcome. She turns to see the Paul Bunyan man has his back to her.

———

Ollie sits on the edge of a narrow and boxy ottoman as Mrs. Forgeron pours a little apple cider into the brown mug. She is frumpy, wearing a bleached apron over an oversized jean fabric dress with her hair in tight spirals. Her smile disappears into her apple cheeks as Mr. Forgeron sits back in his chair with a checkered blanket resting on top of it and rubs his thighs with his hands. In the window, Tre leans against the side of the house and peeks through an open single-pane window in the living room as Mrs. Forgeron places a fresh stick of cinnamon in the mug.

"There," Mrs. Forgeron says, smiling. "Swirl it, and it will bring out the yumminess of the apple."

She walks and sits next to her husband. With non-blinking and bewildered stares, they wait to hear what Ollie will say next. For a couple who lost their only child, they seem to be jubilant and content with their lives, and happy to have a visitor. Ollie drinks down the cider, and Mrs. Forgeron lifts her head as high as the mug goes. Ollie smacks his lips.

"Do you want some more?"

Mrs. Forgeron leans toward the cider kettle. Tre began questioning the Forgerons before Ollie could respond. "Katie has been missing for three years, according to this."

"Katie has been missing for three years, according to this." She repeats, snapping the file against her palm, never taking her eyes off them, hoping to see if she can get a reaction. Ollie knows what he wants to say and says it.

"It's been three years since Katie disappeared..."

"True," Mr. Forgeron says.

"What was she doing before she disappeared?" Tre inquires.

"What was she doing before she disappeared?" Ollie repeats.

Mrs. Forgeron looks at her husband as if waiting for his approval to speak about Katie. Maybe it is a marriage thing, but it's like they are talking to each other, telling each to be careful with their words. Tre watches their lips, hoping they move as the air in the room sucks in. It becomes so dense that slicing it with a knife would be so, difficult, the knife would get stuck in the middle of it. Where can you find an axe when you need one? It's going to be hard to elicit honest responses from these two. Aware, Tre listens.

"We were picking flowers, after all. Then, uh..."

"Katie was very interested in nature." Mr. Forgeron cuts her off.

"What exactly does that mean?" Ollie inquires.

Mr. Forgeron leans forward, resting his elbows on his knees, and says quietly, "She would run into the woods and be gone for days."

"She would run away. Why?"

Silence sinks into the room. Tre's gaze darts back and forth between the Forgerons as they stare blankly at each other. Mrs. Forgeron notices Tre's stare, so Mr. Forgeron turns her chin and directs her gaze back to his with his pinky finger. They make another attempt to ignore her. But Tre saw pain for a split second. It is difficult to lose a child. It's difficult not to have someone in whom you can put all your hopes and dreams, which all the parents on the island do, and it's even

THIS IS NOT USED

more difficult to be controlled by her husband into acting as if everything is perfect and sunny. Tre understands that applying pressure is the best way to deal with the situation, and she will do anything to get the information she needs to find Colby, and now Katie. They will mess up the more she digs the knife into their gut.

"Would you like some more cider, Deputy?" Mr. Forgeron suggests as he pours another cup of cider for Ollie. "This time with two cinnamon sticks."

Tre opens her mouth to speak but then closes it. She requires this to be direct, shocking, and powerful to get them squirming in their seat to talk. "Why would she leave such a beautiful place?"

Tre makes a knock on the windowsill. She sticks her head inside and looks around. Ollie watches Tre as he takes another sip of his cider like he's watching a bad movie. But it piques the Forgeron's interest.

"I don't understand. I mean, Katie has it all. A roof over her head, food on the table, and nature to study. Parents who love her, right Mr. Forgeron? So, what I'm wondering, Mr. Forgeron, is if you did anything to her. Did you hit her? Or anything else? Maybe late at night, or early in the morning."

Mr. Forgeron never looks at her as she makes the most heinous suggestions to him. Tre never gives up. Tre takes out a photograph of Katie. Little does Tre know, Katie's long gown conceals her rebellious side; her baby blue/pink check-ered shirt, and her long, dark hair is full and is so beautiful. I mean look at those eyes. How can you not? It's like she is looking into my soul. Did she ever look into your soul, Mr. Forgeron?"

"Oh, why don't you just shut up."

Mrs. Forgeron snaps her fingers as she rises from her seat and stares directly at Tre. She slowly makes her way, step by step, pointing a skeleton-like finger at Tre with a scowl on her face that could skin a cat. She forces her words out through cinnamon-scented breath as she tries to choke back tears—not tears of pain, but anger.

"How could you? Katie meant everything to me. She would never have—if something was wrong, she would have told me—and there was never anything wrong. We were a happy family. Your father is rolling in his grave because you made him turn his back on you. And I can't say I blame him."

Stepping in front of his wife, Mr. Forgeron prevents her from moving closer. He twists her around so her back is facing Tre. Tre, on the other hand, is not giving up. She's gotten under one person's skin to get them to react. Now it's time to let her wild hairs fly.

"Your first husband died in his sleep, and then you married again a few days later. Katie is probably upset. I'm sure she's pissed. I know I would be."

Mrs. Forgeron begins to cry. Ollie watches like a horror fan as he slurps the rest of his cider. A little dribbles down his chin as he watches like Tre is a serial killer slicing away at her victims.

"Maybe she was changing, growing, maturing. If she ran away, would you blame her? Mr. Forgeron, did you do anything to her, like hit her or anything else? You're not her father, a little cuddle here and there—"

Mrs. Forgeron screams at the top of her lungs, crying and still being held by her husband. "Get out! You get out!"

"First, I am. Second. I'm trying to get to the bottom of why Katie has been missing for so long. So, you can ignore me all you want, but if I find out if and when something happened to her, I will bring the hammer down so hard. You are going to be begging me to help you."

"I gave her everything. She was my everything. I want her back, but I can't because..."

Mrs. Forgeron blurts it out. Mr. Forgeron buries her face inside his chest as she wails, mumbling words neither Tre nor

Ollie can figure out. Mr. Forgeron looks at Ollie and motions toward the window.

"We won't be answering more questions. Please be on your way, deputy. But you are always welcome in our home."

Mrs. Forgeron rises from her husband's chest with a cheerier disposition. "I'll get you a to-go basket."

She walks out. Dumbfounded, Ollie puts the mug down when Tre nudges her head for him to exit out the front door. She watches as Mr. Forgeron rubs the corners of his eyes.

"Gave. Was. Want her back. Whatever you're not telling – you need to. Because I always keep my word. The hammer will hurt, and I will be happy to do it myself."

Mr. Forgeron turns his head and looks at her, but by then she was always walking down the porch. "You wanna make a bet? " He says quietly under his breath to Tre.

Meeting at the same time, Ollie and Tre begin walking down the steps with a basket filled with mixed berry muffins. The Paul Bunyan worker still has his back turned. Ollie looks over his shoulder to see him piling the wood he had hacked against the house. He glances at him, and Ollie naps his neck back.

"I think they know something."

"Yes, they do. But what did she mean when she said she wanted her daughter back? If she hadn't run away."

"Who took her?"

"Exactly," Tre agrees.

Ollie pulls out a large muffin and opens his mouth, anticipating a deep and sweet bite. Right when he is about to take a bite, Tre grabs it. Ollie bites the air and watches her throw the muffin to her side. He wanted it, and he wanted it badly. Then, she grabs the basket and drops it to her side. It lands on its side, the rest of the muffins tumble into the grass, and

Ollie's face falls with disappointment. He really wanted those delicious and fluffy muffins. Tre had no other way of getting his attention. But it worked.

"What now?" Ollie whispers.

"It's the beginning night of the Shredding."

"What's the Shredding?"

"It is the Islanders' start of what mainlanders, or rather, normal people call Christmas."

"But it's March. That's weird."

"You don't know how right you are."

Tre sees a small opening in the woods close to the Forgeron cabin, but not too close for them to see the two turn and enter it. Tre and Ollie set up a stakeout base. After about an hour or two, it pays off. The worker leaves. In addition, the Forgeron couple walk down the porch and down the dirt path toward the main road. Tre pats Ollie and begins to walk out of their hiding spot. Ollie doesn't know what to do.

"What are you doing?" Ollie loudly whispers.

Tre stops half in and half out and looks at him. "I'm going to find out what they know. You go back to the house and begin placing the dates of the other missing Islanders."

"What am I supposed to look for?"

Tre turns back and replies, "Anything."

"Well, that doesn't tell me anything. Boss? Boss?" he calls out. He shakes his head.

Tre trots down the path, hoping she doesn't run into the worker as she looks around. Even if she did, he would ignore her and turn his back on her. She sees it as a win-win situation at this point. She slows down as she approaches the porch. She bobs to the left side of the house and sees no one. She weaves to the right side of the house and finds no one there either. Carefully, she steps on the porch and creaks open the screen door. Trying the front doorknob, Tre is surprised to find it locked.

"Huh. So, not everyone trusts each other around here."

She makes her way around the porch to the window she was at earlier. Lucky for her, it was left open. She crawls through and lands on the wooden laid floor. She walks through the neither hospitable nor spacious living room. A loveseat is against the back of the room near the moveable fireplace, and the two chairs have their own mini-coffee table. All completely clean. But the space between them is a stain, a scratch. She bends down, grazing her finger against it, and she sees both chairs have the same stumpy legs and scratches that are made when they are rocked. Tre assumes the two remaining are the Forgerons while the missing third chair must have been Katie's. If they never wanted to forget her, then why would her chair be put away?

Tre is in the kitchen in a matter of seconds. Freshly cut flowers rest in a vase without water in the center of the dining room table, where three places are set for breakfast, lunch, and dinner. Black lace is placed over one of the plate sets. Tre moves closer for a better look when she notices something is lying in the middle of the plate. A red ribbon ties the silverware together, and it's positioned upside down at the head of the plate. Nervous, her hand trembles as she attempts to lift the black lace. Suddenly, a heavy thud sounds above her as she lifts the black cover. Quickly, she draws her weapon.

She slides up the small, claustrophobic hallway, moving against the curving log wall as she turns the corner. On the opposite wall, dark stains are etched indicting where pictures used to hang. But long nails, which can catch and unravel the end of a shirt or jacket, stick out and are sharp and rusting. Tre hears a second thud, louder and heavier as if struck with a closed fist. She twists her body and points her weapon at the empty bathroom as she rounds the corner at the top of the stairs. There is no mirror where there should be, only the inner gut of a medicine cabinet.

Shifting around quickly, Tre stares down the hallway at a door. As her steps softly touch the floor, she can hear the leather of her boots rub against each other, and the plastic end of her boot laces clings like toasting champagne as they bounce with each step.

Right outside the door, Tre watches a shadow pass as the sunlight shines through the bottom cracks of the door. From inside, dismembered voices mumble. Tre leans her ear against the wood and listens. Although she tries to make out what they are saying, she can only hear a cat purring and a tongue clicking.

"Sheriff's office. Come out with your hands up."

Silence fills the air. The bright sunlight makes Tre's skin turn a jaunty yellow, and the white part of her eyes expands and covers her pupils causing them to fade and end in a crystal-like color. Mysteriously, a female voice calls Tre's name like silk.

"Theresa."

With a blink, Tre's eyes are back to normal. Her skin turns peachy, and her cheeks flush. Without hesitation, she flings the door open. She enters the room—Katie's room.

On the right, a small white dresser set with painted lilies on the drawers has a white nightgown folded neatly into a square and wilted baby's breath resting on top of it.. A simple white kitchen table in the corner is dusted brown with dust, and a pair of slip-on flat shoes are on the lines of the wooden floor. The bed is white with a black blanket lying across it. A small bag nailed to the closed closet door catches Tre's attention. She touches it, and a few droplets of water fall from the edge, landing at her feet. She starts to remember something when another bang startles her.

The loose pane bangs against the window frame once more. That explains the banging she heard. She returns her weapon to its holster as she walks over. She examines the window, noting that it is slightly off track. She smacks it back on track with her fist. It slips back in place.

She turns around and starts looking through Katie's room.

But where to begin? From one glance, nothing screams Katie, let alone a teenage girl. Tre can't find a journal, pictures, drawings, or anything else. It's as if she never existed. She doesn't know what she's looking for, but if she finds it, she'll know.

Tre opens the closet. There is a shift in the water bag. Clicking the long light switch, she sees the closet is empty and stripped of anything of the person it once held. Tre is aware of the sensation. As she shuts the door, the bag lowers to the right. Tre never notices the bag slowly slipping from the nail.

Not knowing how much time she has, Tre gets started. She pulls out the drawers on Katie's dresser. Everything is empty. She looks beneath the bed. It's spotless. Standing up, Tre hears a bump. Beneath her boot, she lowers her gaze to a loose floorboard. She steps off and back onto it, keeping an eye on it as it moves up and down. Tre falls to her knees. She tries to extract it with her fingers, straining, she almost gets a splinter under her fingernails. She then draws a knife from her back pocket. With a swoosh, the blade flips out.

After digging the blade into the corner, she is able to pop out half of the board. On the smooth inner part, the residue of tan wood glue is easy to peel off. Putting her hands on the side of the boards, she looks down only to see a layer of dirt and nothing else. Someone cut it and reattached it, making it appear to be a solid piece. Tre is impressed, she had plenty of hiding places inside her house, but Katie's is far more superior. Reaching her hand inside, she begins to feel around. Not feeling anything yet, she pushes her arm further in.

A set of claws walk towards the area around her hand, unfolding in the dark like a spider's web. They are beautifully black and jagged like barbed wire. With grace, the claws grow in length as they lift above her hand. Anxious for a touch, they shudder, wanting to tickle Tre's hand. Above, Tre is unaware as she tries to look inside as she searches, but the light can't break into the opening well enough to light it up.

Back inside, she flips her hand over and moves, tapping and sliding across the top of the floor's planks. Something is attached to the remaining planks. She braces herself against the floor, grips it tightly, and pulls to release whatever she's found. The claws let the darkness swallow them as the tape ripped.

Rolling from the darkness, a metallic tongue with a waxy finish unrolls and stretches all at once, hovering with pulsating capsules, and inhales Tre's scent. With a curl, the tongue licks the back of her hand. Startles, Tre yanks her hand away and scrambles, hitting the wall behind her, and the tongue returns to the darkness. Tre's hand burns, examining it she notices a long ash mark in a straight line. Finally, the burn diminishes as a thud sounds from the hole. A small box falls onto the dirt floor when she looks inside to see what touches her. But not before she pulls her gun for protection.

Side by side, she places her gun and box on the black blanket on the bed. She looks around to find a Katie's room more like the setting is like a gothic story than a teenage girl's room. Her gaze returns to the bed and to the box which seems to be staring at her. It's impossible to guess what's inside the small blue box. The rotting of the wood has caused the lock to break. Tre finds it odd that this is the only location the wood has rot. She opens the lid, and it falls backward, revealing a diary, a compact, and a flip phone.

She picks up the diary and starts flipping through it, and on the first page, under the title, it says: Katie's Diary." Nothing is dated with numbers, instead Katie used phases of the moon, and her drawings are of animals with names like "Bear," "Squirrel," and other animals. Tre figures these are code names in case someone finds them and wonders who the others are. Let alone punished for going against their parents, the elders, and the island. Her crush on Bear is prominent. Their late-night rendezvous were legendary in her mind, her parents not understanding how she felt being an only child. Next to a drawing of a black mass, Katie tells of a man in black who keeps talking to her in the middle of the night. Also, listening to her chair downstairs, made by her father, rocking back and forth in the middle of the night. On the last page, she talks about adventures with a strange-smelling unnamed man.

"Man with the funny smell."

Tre notices that the remaining pages are empty. She drops it and picks up the deep purple compact. Makeup isn't frowned upon, but it's also not encouraged, especially among teenagers on the island. She takes it out. The powder base has vanished. The silver part is dull, but the mirror underneath the ripped tissue paper is as clean as a whistle. Since arriving, this is the first mirror she has found. Tre looks at herself. She notices she has become paler with bags under her eyes which are growing darker each day since returning to the island. A smudge of smoke on her upper eyelid blends out and disappears upward while wild baby hairs sprout from her hairline and take more auburn tones than her hair. She tries to push it away, but it keeps coming back. She rolls her eyes and looks down. Her reflection hesitates as she moves away from the mirror's view.

Tre moves out of the mirror's field of view. Her reflection, however, remains. Tre's reflection smiles and models inside the mirror. She looks as if she hasn't seen herself in a long time. She never loses the starlike quality she believes she has. Her eyelids cover the top of her eyes, the right side of her mouth curls, and her smile widens, revealing her thinned lips. Tre returns to the compact mirror. And her reflection does the same thing she does.

Tre holds a tie-dye flip phone in her hand. It is the last phone model that was popular before she arrived on the mainland. She opens it and attempts to power it on, but it's dead. She inspects it, checks the charging port, and then looks inside the box. Inside and twisted with a bread tie is the short black charging cord. She places the floorboard back in place and puts everything back inside the box before she smooths out the black blanket, free of wrinkles. She gathers everything and heads downstairs.

Tre plugs the phone in and places it on one of the end tables near a rocking chair. Tre hopes the phone will do something since it's been a long time since it's been on. Near the dark corner, she gazes out the window to make sure she's still alone. Surprisingly, the phone powers up.

Tre begins to go through it with little battery left. As she scrolls, she recognizes the contact names from Katie's diary, Bear and Squirrel. She dials the number for Bear. The phone rings. After the fourth ring, it goes to voicemail. So, someone has it. That's a good sign. Back at the main screen, she brings up the photo app. As she goes through it, she discovers a multitude of selfies of Katie posing with peace signs, the duck lips, and hand on the hip. Squinting, Tre looks closer to one picture. Tre explodes with frustration and anger. She slams it shut, then clutches it in her trembling fist.

"Son of a bitch."

CHAPTER 11
CRAWFISH DADDY AND THE KIDS

"ARE you going to tell me? Or do I get to beat it out of you?"

Tre yells as she charges down the dock, clutching Katie's phone.

Finkle emerges from the tons of shrimp, crawfish, and fish surrounding him on the dock. He squints his eyes as he notices Tre boarding.

"Sure. Come on board."

"Screw you."

"Oh, let me, Sheriff."

Finkle, being the smartass that he is, closes his eyes and places a crawfish on his left temple. He begins to hum Amazing Grace as he slightly inclines toward the sky. Rolling her eyes, Tre sighs. It doesn't matter how old Finkle gets. He still makes Tre feel stupid and insignificant. But this time, she has a gun. And she will not hesitate to use it, as she did before.

The crawfish uses its claws to snip at his brow, and Finkle winces in surprise, as if Karma is laughing at him. Tre chuckles and leans in close as he hops around on the dock, making other fishermen look and begin to gag at them. Finkle is still Finkle, just on a different day.

"Serves you right for lying to me. It's your punishment for lying to me."

After a few seconds, he takes off the crawfish. He touches his wet and dirty glove to his eyebrow, trying to figure out if he is bleeding or not. He can't tell, of course. He looks to Tre for an answer. But it may not be the one he wants at this point since she's mad, pissed, frustrated—either way, she has a vengeful side, and for her, the crawfish did it for her.

"Is it bad?"

"Not as bad as I wish it was."

"What in the hell are you talking about?"

As Tre goes through Katie's phone, Finkle keeps touching the crawfish snip, checking to see if it's bleeding, which it isn't. Finkle is irritated by Tre, as evidenced by his blank expression, and parted lips. After a few seconds, she extends her hand in front of his face. It's of him and Katie on his dock in the middle of the lake.

"Would you mind explaining?"

"It's Katie Forgeron."

Tre is taken aback by Finkle's carefree attitude and nonchalant voice. She only looks at him, wide-eyed. She shakes her head back and forth as her hair blows in the wind. "And?"

Taking off his gloves, Finkle copies her movements, and says, "And?"

"Why are you in a picture with a missing girl?"

"Keep your voice down."

"Don't tell me what to do, Jacob. I know you have been traveling to the mainland for years. And it looks like you've had visitors."

A few fishermen on the other side of the dock exchange glances as they pack it with new supplies and begin to whisper in Lone. The Lone Language consists of tongue clicks, with short clicks representing jokes and long clicks are entire conversations. The longer they click, the worse it will be for the fishermen. Click or not, gossip can ruin a fisherman and their business. When Finkle notices it, he dashes over and grabs the phone from her grasp.

"Shut up and fuck off. Please?"

Finkle tries not to be too obvious when he looks at the fishermen, who are still staring and pretending to work. Tre notices them as she looks over her shoulder. Of course, they quickly turn away. But it makes no difference to her. A bolt of lightning strikes her. If she is to get her answers, she must show the fishermen and Finkle that she means business.

"I suggest you talk to me. Or we can talk down at the Marshall's station."

"That isn't a threat if you mean it to be. Spence is a fucking joke."

"He may be, but if he and everyone else find out you stepped on the mainland, that would make you like me. Wouldn't it?"

Finkle doesn't like what she said. He has a reputation—not a good one, but one nonetheless. He's one of the best fishermen on the island. If that gets ruined, he's ruined. He hits her in the middle of her chest with Katie's phone and steps back. He stares at her head-to-toe, then smirks.

"You know you've turned into a real bitch."

"As far as I'm concerned, I'll do anything to keep my job."

Finkle laughs and points and says, "Your job? I bet."

Before he walks into his boat's cabin, he throws his gloves at her, hitting her in the face. The fisherman across the way burst out laughing. Tre's hair flutters across her face as she returns her gaze to the men, who walk away, clicking short clicks. What Finkle just did will be all over the island in no time. Dropping the gloves over the side of the boat, she heads inside.

Finkle is drinking a beer at the small bar. He finishes it and lets the bottle fall and roll to the floor. He appears to have lost his facial color, like a child caught with their hand in the cookie jar. He looks at Tre.

"Do you want to know why I went to the mainland?"

"Are you talking about Katie Forgeron?"

"I was there checking on you."

"Here we go. How about some woe is me, Jacob," Tre exclaims, throwing her arms up in the air.

"It's true."

"Bullshit."

"I made a promise to Mom before she died. I made sure your letters got to her. I wanted her to know about you, so I never took them out of the bag I collected."

Tre points her finger and narrows her eyes as she searches Finkle's heart, not for the compassion he keeps displaying. But for the darkness of these lies he's telling her. She paces to keep her anger in check. Finkle has never had the right to bring up her—or their mother.

"All she ever wanted to know was that you were okay. Were you in good health? Were you homeless? What did you do? Did you ever have a good man in your life? She was interested in anything and everything I could find out. So, I told her."

Tre doesn't want to hear this. To her, Finkle is shit. His words are nothing more than word vomit. She stops pacing and places her in the air as she pushes against the air, wanting him to stop.

"Please, please, please. Don't pretend you did me a favor."

Finkle takes a step forward. Each Finkle sibling stands in a different corner of the couch, kicking cans and beer bottles like the first time Tre visited, proving he never cleans.

"I didn't do it for you."

"How about we stop trying to repair this sibling thing and you tell me the truth. Why are you with Katie Forgeron?"

"The truth?"

"Yeah. I know it's hard, but I think you can do it. Just this one time. Come on. You can do it."

Finkle doesn't like the way she hits her leg like he's going to get a treat for sitting or balancing on his hind legs. The sibling thing what even is that? They haven't had a sibling relationship for years–what's the point in repairing something neither of them cares about it.

"If I tell you will you hurry and wrap this case up and go back to the mainland?"

"It will be my pleasure. I don't want to be here any longer than I have to."

"Fine. I have been going to the mainland for years. This is true. Besides to check on you, I have been importing and exporting."

"Importing and exporting? What?"

Finkle pops the cap off another beer and flops on the couch, crushing the cans and taking a big swig. Tre stays where she is, waiting for a good answer or the one he is trying to think of to silence her.

"Sometimes it was candy or something similar. Snack foods, you know. It may sound ridiculous, but it's one thing we don't have here for the kids. Then the teenagers found out about me. Of course, I kept it under wraps—we kept it under wraps. So, we traded a few things."

"Money."

"The more money I made, the more inventory I bought, like small televisions, radios, and cell phones—so they could talk. Then they wanted to go to the mainland with me for reasons other than the internet. Which they loved, by the way."

"Who doesn't."

"When one of the teens got caught with their phone, they never gave me up. So, I rewarded them I guess you would say. I threw parties. Out in the middle of the lake. Where none of the Islanders could hear us. That's the picture with Katie. It was her birthday. Her parents didn't want to celebrate it like she wanted. So, her friends did. On my boat."

That's when it hit Tre that the names in Katie's phone, Bear, Squirrel, and other animal names were her friends. There has to be a way for them to contact Finkle. She opens the phone and shows him the names.

"Let me guess, you're Owl."

"It's not the name I would have picked for myself. I wanted something like Craw Daddy."

"Right. What about Colby Morel?"

Finkle leans over the bar's side and picks another beer from the small refrigerator. Popping the top, he takes a sip. Settling back down, he shakes his head and runs his fingers through his hair.

"When was the last time you saw him?"

"A few hours before he went missing."

Tre's mouth drops, "Are you serious?"

"I swear he was fine. All he wanted was to go for a dip in the water. That night I took him out, we drank, and he went swimming."

"Are you trying to look like a perve?"

"What! No!"

"Because I guarantee you others are going to see it that way. A middle-aged man hanging with teens – in the middle of the night. Now their missing," Tre claps her hand together, "Wake up, Jacob."

"It's been a hard season. I needed the money."

Finkle lays the beer on the coffee table. Tre walks around in a small circle, racking her mind. She knows she has to do the right thing and bring him in for more questioning, but it's so hard. Even though they don't have a relationship or the bond they once had, he's still her brother. And she knows Marshall Spence will rake him over the coals and enjoy watching his flesh split before the elders get him. She walks over and drops down beside him. For a few moments, no one looks at or speaks to each other as the clock on the wall ticks.

"Did anyone see you with Colby?"

"No."

"Are you sure?"

"Yep."

"Fuck me."

Tre returns to silence and takes the beer bottle from the coffee table. She sips the drink. Finkle takes a sip after she hands it to him.

"Okay. You keep as low a profile as possible, and I mean low. No more trips to the mainland and no more parties. Got it?"

"I've got a job to do, Tre."

"Give some more responsibility to Isaiah, He'll love it."

"I would, but he hasn't been here in a few days."

"Where is he?"

"You're asking the wrong person."

Tre gets up as she says, "Figure it out. He couldn't have gone far."

"And what are you going to do?"

"Figure out how to keep your name out of this."

"You'd do that for me?"

"No. I'm doing it for mom. Just like you did."

Finkle leans up and says, "If you hear anything about Isaiah, you'll let me know, right?"

"I will. If you have the—desire to go back out and play— please don't, and remember…"

"They're always watching."

"Who?"

"Never mind. I will."

"How did you make it out there in the water in the dark? I thought you hated the dark."

"I do. It was always light out there. With the lanterns and all."

"And all…yeah."

Tre leaves, but not before she swipes a bottle of scotch off the small square table hidden in the corner of Finkle's houseboat. Finkle slouches back in his couch and finishes the beer with a loud burp..

"That's my baby sister."

CHAPTER 12
ISAIAH WALKS THROUGH THE SMALL PATH

ISAIAH IMAGINES what everything sounds like as he walks the same path his ancestors the Dolson Twin did. The birds singing nature's chorus surrounds him. The water splashes against the side of the boat, and the birds flap their wings, chatting and chirping about what the blue sparrow did to the red robin the night before. The roughness of the rope tightens as Isaiah pulls, allowing it to slide in his small, calloused palms as he looks down and admires the knot. He smiles to himself.

Tying knots can be complicated, but not for Isaiah. As a child, it was the way he communicated with his parents and other relatives—after all, the entire family was deaf. Sign language was never an option, nor did any of them care since it wasn't taught. So, they came up with their own language. Knots. Square knots were for dinner, cloves knots passed gossip, bowlines knots were arguments, and sheer bends knot reminded each other how much they loved one another. The best and most knot seen was one they came up with, a shoelace knot with shredded edges, It was for whenever one of the Islanders slowed their speech or mouth to help them understand. They were deaf, not stupid. No one got it, but it made for delightful story time at night before bed.

Jobs were hard to come by for Isaiah. The most memorable one was when he was a shelf stocker at Quills. The manager always stopped his own job, which was nothing except sitting at his desk and seeing how far he could lean back on his two legs. He always fell flat on his back. Or telling the female cashier how his family is one of the founding families of Pine Island. They aren't. He's not. He always wanted to make sure he was important, because he believed he was. He was nothing more than a bending and eventually snapped piece of pine straw that no one noticed. But when Isaiah would be stocking, the manager always found something to be upset about.

The store manager had the disease of perfection. He constantly yelled at the top of his lungs. He would go on and on as customers look on, interest and whispers. All Isaiah did was smile. And was relieved he couldn't hear the store manager rant and rave right before he got fired.

When Isaiah notices a shadow above him, he turns around, shielding his eyes from the sun's glare. Finkle takes a white envelope from his back jeans pocket. He gives it to Isaiah.

"This is your cut. I know it's not what I promised, but it's better than nothing."

Isaiah opens the envelope and counts five one-hundred bills. He smiles and taps the envelope on Finkle's chest as he steps around him. Finkle's face sinks because he knows he is a piece of shit liar. He looks over his shoulder as Isaiah walks down the boat dock, happy with the money because it will help his family. Finkle pulls out a wad of hundreds, exactly five hundred-dollar bills. He pursues his lips together. He just lied to his best friend. He stuffs them back into his pocket. Never saying a word, he turns and heads back onto his boat. Dashing back out with a small lantern, Finkle runs down the dock. He stops himself as his boot hovers over the patch of grass below it. The sun is descending quicker than he expected, and he watches as Isaiah vanishes behind the curve toward the main road.

"Better make it before the sun does."

The main road is the only way Islanders travel to get home. As they pass each other, they nod and exchange smiles of contentment. To them, it's not odd how no one ever speaks as they walk down the halls of their non-existent school. In groups of four, people turn down small paths toward their houses and their waiting families. They walk down the street in silence. They are not holding hands, their arms are not intertwined, nor do they joke with each other.

As the sun begins to set, Isaiah decides to take a shortcut home. Finkle has always warned him to stay on the black pavement because it is the fastest way, but tonight he changes his mind. With his money in hand, he quickly darts into the woods. He is heading toward Quills to buy something special for dessert. Maybe rosemary and pecan crackers with plum jelly, banana pudding with crushed cookies on top, or his favorite zucchini bread with walnuts and cinnamon.

Crushing the pine straw under his sandals, he steps carefully over the hidden tree stumps. The birds chatter in the branches like they're sharing an eerie story as the radiant blue-sky colors with pink and gray hues. He walks past a hunter's cage to see that it's popped, but nothing is inside. A slight breeze rushes through, chilling his bare arms and grazing his cheeks as if licking them. Without warning, a pinecone hits his back.

Swiftly, he turns. No one is there. Not a rustle in the bushes, nothing. He shrugs it off. After a few steps, another pinecone hits his back once again. He stops. He believes someone is playing with him. When a third pinecone whizzes past his head, the pricks on it scratch the curve of his ear, and he takes another step forward. Bright red blood sprinkles the tip of his index finger and paints his inner fingernail. He twirls around.

A muffled sound emerges from his mouth as if he is calling out to whomever it is. Still wanting to make his point, he picks up a long piece of green and brown bark from the ground. Knowing it will break, he still tries to make a knot. It fails.

In the distance, the sun sets, and a shadow soothes itself over the woods. His eyes widen as he sees a figure in the darkness weaving its way toward him. Fast. He tumbles backward over a tree root and lands on his butt. A small pain hits hard as his tailbone and the root collide. But that's the least of his problems.

Gracefully and delicately, the shadow slows its pace and bends down to Isaiah. A dribble of blood slowly appears as a thin slice is made right below his cheekbone. He stares into pure darkness, looking for anything as the darkness begins to engulf him. To cool his sweaty bangs, a long exhale blows them back and wrinkles his button-up white shirt. He closes his eyes because the spit he feels is hot like fire as it hits his skin, cauterizing the freshly made scratch. The treetops are filled with crows, each one watching with intrigue and in silence. But he isn't going to stay.

As fast as his legs will take him, he makes his way through the woods, scrambling to his feet with every trip he makes. He can't call for help. He's on his own. He should have listened to Finkle. He should have taken Finkle's word to heart.

When he looks back, he sees darkness galloping after him. The tiny light left is in front of him. Bearing down on his feet, he pumps his legs as best he can, barely touching the ground. Just in front of him, the main road is right through the small, overgrown trees. All he must do is not look back. On all sides of him, darkness breaks apart, swallows the gray light, and heads toward the orange and pink hues. He turns his head to the left. With a dislocation in its neck, darkness lunges toward him and he trips.

Screams don't have a sound to Isaiah, but if they did, it would be his blood washing the black pavement as his fingernails become the gravel the Islanders will step on in the morning, afternoon, and evening.

CHAPTER 13
MOM'S LETTER AND SOMETHING IS WRONG WITH OLLIE

THE EDGE of Tre's finger circles the rim of the empty whisky glass. As she leans her chin on the back of the chair, she stares back at the letters she wrote to her mother from the Mainland. Sabine gave them to her for a reason. It's like they are playing strange game of who will blink first. With a quick grip, she wraps her slender fingers around the bottle and sloppily pours a glass. Tre lost. She shoots a shot and pours another before the first one even has a chance to slide down her throat. After she slams down the glass, she lets out a long "ah" and gets up. She walks around and looks back and forth between the wall, floor, and letters. She doesn't know how to feel or what to do.

The letters beam at her like children, daring her to open them and remember what life was like during her years she was on the island. She chuckles to herself. She flips the chair around and sits in it backward. Leaning on her back, she breathes inside her folded arms. Her hot air, hard and heavy, begins to move her hair around. Suddenly, she slaps the glass off the table. It lands on the floor after hitting the wall. After taking a large gulp of the scotch straight from the bottle, she sets it down and pulls the letters toward her. She rips the red ribbon, which releases the stack as they slide back onto the table.

Walking her fingers through the unopened envelopes, Tre's face is empty as she picks a random one out. She peels it open and pulls out a three-folded letter. Written in the right corner is the number fifteen. Tre used to keep track of how many letters she sent each month—a record of how many times she tried to contact; not to beg for forgiveness for leaving, but to have her understand why. Ripping open the first letter, she can already hear echoes of her voice when she wrote it that sunny day in the rundown motel on the mainland.

Dear Mom,

Day fifteen on the mainland, dating is such an issue for me. I want to. I really do. The mainland men are very different from us. They talk a lot about themselves. I don't know if it's the way they were raised or because of social media, which is very prevalent today. I try to listen, but most of the time I am planning what I'm going to eat the next day.

Tre rips through multiple letters. The flaps of the envelope's scraps fall to the floor.

Dear Mom,

Day seventy-six on the mainland. It was the first time I thought about coming home. I can't do this. The academy is a lot harder. The *brochure looked so easy. I have always been a runner, but they want something else. Like Superman, which I am not. My partner is nothing more than a jerk who sees me as a weak person. But I am not giving up. I am going to prove him wrong.*

Sitting in the dining room, Tre chugs a bottle of scotch.

Dear Mom. Dear Mom. Dear Mom. Dear. Mom.

Day one hundred and two, day one hundred and twelve, two hundred and forty-nine.

Tre leans back, brings a letter closer to her face, and slams it back down on the stack. She scrambles through it and picks one out.

I thought I knew what I wanted. How can I stand there and agree to be with someone I didn't love?

Tre shakes the table as she places her boots on the table's edge. Stretching her arm down to the floor, she tries to pick up one of the nine letters on the floor that tumbled down after she moved to get comfortable.

She misses a few times but finally gets one. Shaking the paper, she begins to read after focusing her eyes. Almost crossed, tired, and drunk, her eyes blur and clear many times as she reads.

Merry Christmas and Happy New Year, Mom. My tree is bare once again with the exception of the empty boxes I wrapped for you,

Jacob, and Dad. I didn't know what y'all wanted, so I didn't...I know I can't send them. But I have a thousand times since being here. How are you? Why haven't you written back to me? I miss you, Mommy.

Hours have passed, and Tre continues to read each one, remembering what, where, and why she wrote it, but she greatly needs to hear her words or finally let it go so she can do the job she is there to do. Finkle appears at her bedroom door, but it feels like he's hovering over her shoulder as he shakes his head at her while she highlights her memory like a spotlight.

"You had to do it to her, didn't you, Tre?" Finkle says as he vanishes and walks up the stairs.

From the crack in the door, Finkle watches as Tre hurries back and forth from her dresser to bed. A duffle bag is half full of clothes. He carefully pushes her door open. Hearing the creak, Tre knocks her duffle bag onto the floor, stands, and smiles.

"Hey," she says with a nervous smile.

"Please tell me you're not doing what I think you're doing?" Finkle asks.

Acting dumb, Tre scrunches her face, confused, and narrows her eyes. Finkle stands in the doorway, folds his arms, and can't wait to hear what she comes up with.

"I am not doing anything." She notices Finkle's motion to the edge of the duffle bag poking out, "Oh, this. No, it's not. I was packing them for cha-char-charity. I was thinking we should start one. Don't you think…"

"I don't care what you do, just don't break her heart, She's fighting for you down there, and if you leave…"

"I can't take it here, Jacob. I want more. And I'm not going to get it here."

"Don't do it. Because you know what's going to happen."

Tre walks around the room and puts her hands on her head. She crouches down. She does jumping jacks. Then she shuffles through the letters, watching some fall, and picks one.

Tre sits at her Sheriff's desk, vigorously writing as she holds her breath with every slant and curve she makes. Once done, she places it inside the envelope and tosses it in the mail-out pile. It reads **CASS FINKLE** on the front.

She gets up and walks to the window. She stares out, and a single tear rolls down her flushed cheek. The sun beams down and reflects Pine Island in the distance, teasing and staring back at her. She scoffs and walks away, leaving the sound of her mouth loud and ringing in her office.

Tre drops her head on the table as she crumples another letter in her hand, squeezing it as hard as she can until her knuckles turn white. Suddenly, she stands and tosses the letter across the room.

All I ever wanted was more.

Tre rakes everything off the table. The rest of the letters and envelopes flutter down onto the ground. She trips on the chair's legs and almost falls.

That is the difference between us. You settled for love, happiness, and a family. I'm not ready.

She falls on her buttocks. She scrambles up, picking up the chair and throwing it. It hits the ground.

Can you honestly tell me you have been happy? Because there's always something happening. Whether it's fighting about me, Jacob, or, the council…the council is horrible. Dad said they made our lives better, but they didn't.

Tre kicks another chair and pushes another away from the table.

I know you're thinking they know better because they have been around since the island's establishment. But come on Mom. They don't know how we feel. They never will. I can't accept it.

She grabs the head of the scotch bottle, twirls it, and lets it go. It shatters against the wall. The rest of the scotch slides down the wall, and the pieces fall. Heavily breathing, Tre makes her way out and toward the stairs.

I didn't, I won't…

Tre stomps up the stairs.

End up like you.

Her mother's letters and an empty bottle of scotch can be seen through the broken glass. Tre is slumped over on the table, passed out, in one of the chairs. She scares herself by snoring, which startles her and causes her to jump while wearing an envelope on her forehead. She looks around, confused. The last thing she remembers was upstairs. How did she end up at the table again?

Sunlight streamed in through the windows, piercing the sheer curtains. Tre tries to shield her eyes, realizing too late that one of her envelopes, which contained one of her mother's letters, was stuck to her head. She yanks it off when she does. Then, of course, she feels the effects of the sun's morning brightness.

She bumps the bottle, causing it to fall. The ruffles on the outside roll like a jagged pill as it lands, cutting a smooth patch of soft and delicate tissue—not the most pleasant sensation in the world.

Slow and careful, she makes her way up the last few steps until she hits the top stairs. There she holds herself up as her head spins. Her stomach knocks and rubs its hands together, anticipating a puke parade. If she thinks about the royal throne, she will likely knight it before she even makes it to her bedroom.

Determined to make it to her bed for a few extra hours—or at least ten minutes—of sleep before her workday begins, she slowly makes her way in front of Ollie's door, hesitating every few seconds and stomach churning. A dark figure catches the corner of her left eye.

Ollie is usually excited about his day on the job. Sometimes he can be overly anxious to catch the bad guys, as he likes to call them. He's been watching episodes of COPS along with Law & Order—not just one, but every episode ever made. But...

Four hawks soar slowly above the tree line through the window, forming a perfect circle that people wish they could draw freehand. In the glare, Ollie appears in a trance as he stares out. Each feather flutters loudly, making him wince in pain as the slice in the air hits his ears.

Tre walks in and stops. Pushing up her sleeves, she turns her head. Ollie is inches away from the window while standing in his long green and blue checkered pajama pants and a single white t-shirt.

He tilts his head to the side, revealing his unmistakably pale face. As he looks at her, the whiteness of his eyes vibrates, and his pupil dilates.

"It spends the day walking through the woods and watching the house. I see its mouth move, but it never speaks," he says as Tre approaches, returning his gaze to the window. "Until the evening. That's when it starts speaking to me. However, I see it everywhere I go."

"Some people have strange reactions to this place."

"It's voice is calm, but I hear something inside it pleading with me to save it."

Tre stands next to him as he stares out the window. She tries to pinpoint the exact location where he is staring. She is unable. The land is too large for Ollie, and he shakes. She turns to face him. His lips are parched, and he's perspiring. But she is blind to what he sees. Dew slides along the glass, transforming into a haunting face with narrow beadlike eyes, horns extending from the center of its head, and teeth drawing down from the tip of its fangs, like a predatory animal about to bite into the warm and peachy taste of flesh. As it moves around, Ollie smiles. The beautiful horror of what it does to him astounds and enthralls him.

"It demands me as much as I want it."

As frost forms on the window, Ollie takes a step back into the shadowy part of his room. As Tre leans in closer, his breath turns to white smoke. She watches as the sun becomes obscured by storm clouds rolling in like fresh dough. Ollie's breathing is deep, he sucks in his cheeks and exhales fog. From behind, he looks Tre down. He's tense. The bones in his neck twist and snap, sending a twinge of pain down his right side. He shudders. He doesn't hate him, but he does turn it on. His hand hovers just above Tre's wild strands as he reaches out to touch her hair, inhaling her dry shampoo and alcohol scent. His eyes go black as sunken cheeks tighten around his facial bones, and his teeth decay and fall onto the small area carpet beneath him.

"You would tell me if something were wrong, right?" Tre asks.

Never noticing the frost, Tre continues to follow the tree line outside.

"How could you leave us like you did? I want the truth Theresa Marie Finkle."

Tre stops as her eyes divert from the tree line to the floor. She knows he is staring at her. Ollie's voice is gruff and declares a sense of ownership. Ollie has never addressed her by her full first name. He had no idea until he arrived here. Tears automatically fill her eyes as she listens to a familiar voice talk to her.

"You are selfish. I expected more from you. My only daughter."

Ollie's voice deepens with a grunt, just like when he was

disappointed in her. She twists around. Ollie continues to stare at her without blinking. His eyes grow dimmer, and their whiteness turns to shadows. Tre, taken aback, begins to place her hand on his shoulder. She realizes he is sleep-walking after some hesitation. She remembers if she scares him, he may react violently.

Ollie closes his eyes as Tre rests her hand on his shoulder. He wakes up gasping and furrows his brows. Tre can feel the tenseness and contorting muscles inside his shoulder where she rests her hand. She squeezes it slightly. Ollie shuts his eyes. He inhales causing his shirt to band against his body like rubber that shows his rib cage. He never exhales. Silence controls the room. He gasps, and his body jerks like a poster dropping in the middle of the night. Tre jumps backward and leans against the window as her stomach falls to the floor and her heart leaps inside her mouth.

"Tre, why are you in my room?" He looks around, perplexed. He looks down and realizes he's still in his paja-mas. He takes a step back, embarrassed. "What happened?"

"You were sleepwalking."

"Did I do or say something strange? Because I used to do that."

"No. You didn't. You just stood there."

"Thank you, God. That's something I haven't done in years. But it was the first time I didn't do anything. My mother could tell you where she found me."

Ollie laughs after a minute. He takes a deep breath of relief and exhales it. Tre wipes her tears away, trying to forget what happened as she calms down.

"She once found me naked in a garbage can."

"Crazy."

"Well, I better get ready for work. Are you sure you're alright, boss?"

"Yeah. I'm fine."

Ollie walks out of his room, still laughing at himself, and

closes the door. Tre is baffled while she is still leaning against the windowpane. Behind her, a shadow passes and darkens the light. It catches her off guard, and she quickly turns around. She sees nothing, especially since she is on the second floor. She looks up at the sky. It's clear. She follows the line of trees in the distance once again. As she walks out of Ollie's bedroom, she sighs and grabs the corners of her eyes.

"I just want to go home."

A hawk slams into the window which causes the frost crack.

CHAPTER 14
NOW YOU HEAR ME

AUGUSTE ESCOFFIER ONCE SAID, "Good food is the foundation of genuine happiness." For Islanders, mealtimes can solve anything, savory, sweet, or sour.

Tre picks at her untouched turkey sandwich and pushes the loose chips on the plate. Slurping his potato soup, Ollie listens as Tre discusses the missing children and how they may be related to the Dolson Sisters, Katie Forgeron, and The Woman in the Woods, of whom she has yet to tell Ollie that is really Sadie. She taps on the table to get his attention as he hurls one spoonful of soup after another into his mouth.

Dribbles of white sauce dribbles off his chin. Tre raps on the table, shaking the water in front of Ollie. The vibration creates a small whirlwind inside, splitting the milky discoloration from the lemon juice from the lemon wedge on the side of the glass. He can hear the whirlwind's whip and the cling of the trapped loose lemon seeds circling out of control. A splash of potato soup splashes back into the bowl. Tre's hand slowly lifts, and the knock from her knuckles echoes and shakes the silverware on the opposite side of their table.

He turns his head. An old man in a red hunter's wool cap takes a bite of his BLT on wheat. The crunch of the bacon hides the sogginess of the bread due to the slipperiness of the tomatoes and the gobs of mayonnaise, which sound like a sponge filled with holes of soap.

Tre waves her hand in front of his face. "Earth to Ollie?"

"Maybe they are all related," Ollie replies as he wipes his chin.

"That's what I was saying."

"Oh. Right. You did."

Tre hits her hands on the table and leans in close to him. "Okay, what's wrong with you?"

"I don't know what you mean."

"That is what I mean. You are talking and acting weird. When you stare off into space, you look like Jack Torrance on a bender. So, what gives?"

Ollie lowers his head and tries to avoid her glare.

"I don't know. ever since we got here. I, I..."

A waitress dressed in a baby blue 50's waitress uniform with her hair in a bun and a small white hat placed in it like a tiara arrives. She takes Ollie's plate and surprises him with a large slice of apple pie. The crust's bottom layer is thick and shines. Large chunks of green and red apples fill the middle with yummy stickiness, which hugs each slice and holds warm, in preparation for that first bite of yumminess. The top layer is solid and tight, a spiral with a caramel drizzle in a perfect curl on the flaky top layer. Following that, it's in the wooden bowl with a medium-sized scoop of vanilla ice cream, melting from the heat and cold against the bowl. Ollie's eyes widen.

"We didn't order this," Tre emphasizes.

"Here you are, Deputy Boden. Just a little something from us here in the diner. For—well, for being such a wonderful guest and trying to solve these awful missing person cases."

Ignoring Tre, the waitress continues. She adds another scoop of vanilla ice cream on top. Taking a big fork full, Ollie closes his eyes and moans. It's as if he has never tasted anything so delectable. The waitress's apple cheeks spring out as she smiles.

"There's more where that came from."

"I could get used to this."

The waitress walks off. Ollie offers Tre some as he shoves another bite into his mouth. She dismisses it, then notices the men at the table across from them are staring. At first, she thinks they are looking at her. But she follows their eye line and realizes they are not looking at her, but at Ollie. A nickel falls into the slot, knocking the slide down and landing in the coin collector. An index finger hits one-sixty-six, and a song from the 1950s bounces through the air. They never look away until he finishes every bite of the pie and even the melted ice cream. As Tre shifts in the booth, an uneasy feeling creeps up her spine.

Islanders sit talking and sipping steamy coffee. Glasses cling. Plates slide down the silver counter from the kitchen, and a waitress clicks another ticket on the roundabout and spins it. The order tickets make a whirling sound as muddy clumps from the footprints of a pair of shoes make imprints on the jukebox, which end at the bar counter. A chunks of grass and mud drops from his leg hair as he sits on the stool bar, catching and hanging before sliding off the silver bar and onto the floor. Grayish in color, the mud is attached to long strands of black hair on the legs of a man with shredded shorts, especially at the ends, and his shirt is dusted red. Isaiah licks his dry lips.

Slightly offbeat, he taps his foot and rocks back and forth to the drumbeat of the song. He cracks his neck to the singer's wavy inflection of her voice. He puckers his still rough and dry lips to prepare them as he whistles loudly like a pair of yodeling windchimes, which pair perfectly.

Tre, like the others, comes to a complete stop. From the glass to the table and onto the floor, water overflows from the water pitchers and mixes with the coffee. Islanders' mouths freeze in the middle of a bite and stunned eyes stare.

Beginning in the back, a wave of silence washes over everyone and everything they were doing. The men in the backstop mid-sip and place their hands on them to muffle the noise of the coffee inside. The waitress comes to a halt as she holds a dirty dish tray. A crumpled napkin rolls off the top. Isiah grabs it quickly. On the large stovetop, the cook in the back reduces the sizzle of the bacon. The teen corner gossip comes to a halt, and one holds their soda in their mouth, feeling the burn from the frizzies as they try not to swallow. Even new customers stop at the door open with a slight crack. More people step up and look through the window. Everyone watches, never speaking and too afraid to move.

Isaiah ends the song on an upbeat note with a high-pitched whistle. The jukebox becomes deafeningly quiet. As he adjusts himself on the stool, it squeaks. Everybody is holding their breath. An older woman sits in the booth and continuously blinks, waiting for her cataracted eyes to focus on the blurry figure in front of her.

"I guess I have some catching up to do."

Short and throaty, Isaiah's laugh fills the dinner as he pushes off the edge of the counter, s ending the stool and himself into a circle. All the Islanders, inside and out, begin to roll out in laughter at his joke. Tre is shocked. Isaiah can not only hear, but he can speak. Since she can remember, he has never spoken except for a few sounds. Intensely watching him, she watches his stare grow darker. It's like he's already chewing on her soul and spitting it out the longer they keep their gaze. Something is wrong.

Tre stands across the street, watching as everyone acts as if they have witnessed a miracle or had their prayers answered by an invisible angel. But who is to blame? Who made this happen? Finkle walks up the sidewalk on his tiptoes, curious to see if the rumors are true. He tries everything he can to get closer, but he can't. Tre believes that not only is she blocked out, but he is also purposefully blocked out.

"Isaiah."

Finkle and Isaiah immediately embrace, and their smiles are as big as Pine Island. They're not just two old friends, but a family who speak a secret language only they understand. However, this time it will be in a language everyone will understand, not only Isaiah. Ollie looks around as he emerges from the diner and meets Tre's gaze. He rushes over.

He smiles as he walks over, clutching his full stomach and a light brown wide-brimmed hat. Tre steps alongside him and leans against the dark green wooden bar. She returns her attention to Isaiah as Marshall Spence approaches and embraces him. Ollie is equally enthralled, and he keeps looking back and forth at Tre as she is emotionless.

"What are you thinking?"

"That's a rhetorical question."

"Why is that?"

"You'd think that for someone with so many questions, you'd be able to answer some of them yourself."

"Sorry, boss."

"No, I am. Don't you think it's odd for someone to get their hearing back after being deaf all their life?"

"The Islanders are saying it's a miracle."

"And since I was a child, I nor anyone else here has been taught about miracles."

"Oh, come on. There has to be something you believed in as a child."

"I saw more of the Devil than I did God here, and most of it was in the dark."

Ollie turns to her slowly and looks at her with so many questions. Tre's afraid to look back because she doesn't want to remember, let alone explain. Marshall Spence crawls onto a small chair made of logs and quiets the Islanders down as they talk and continue to do what Tre sees. They are welcoming back Isaiah by shaking his hand, patting him on the back, and the women lean in for hugs.

"Why are they welcoming him back? He never went anywhere. As far as I know."

"Ladies and gentlemen, tonight is the beginning of Shredding. And we know what that means. We are going on The Run, well, some of us are. I have a feeling there is going to be one eligible bachelor who will be running for his life," Marshall Spence chuckles as he circles his finger toward Isaiah.

Everyone pats him on the back and laughs at the not so funny joke Marshall Spence made.

"All right. Let's sit down and decorate," Marshall Spence yells with excitement.

"What's The Run? It sounds like fun," Ollie exclaims.

"Nice rhythm, Deputy."

Levi walks up, happy and interested in what is happening with Tre and Ollie.

"Thanks. I have always had a knack for beats," Ollie says as he drums the air embarrassingly. "To answer your question, The Run is an old tradition."

"It's barbaric."

Tre steps from the wooden pole and shakes her head, saying, "Am I the only one who is finding that Isiah's hearing is back a little fucked up? We have two teens missing that I know of and a woman in the woods, who was murdered, brutally, and no one on this god forsaken island gives two flying fucks. All they want to do is run in the forest and marry someone instead of finding them."

"They are just happy for him," Ollie points out.

"No, you're right. We need to keep our eyes on the prize

and that's the missing people. But you aren't going to be able to make them look when it's the Shredding."

"This is crazy. I'll do it myself."

Tre walks off as Finkle walks up.

"Am I missing something? I mean my best friend just got his hearing back."

"And you don't think it's weird?" Tre hollers as she walks further away.

CHAPTER 15
THE RUN

LOVE COMES FIRST. The innocent crush, peering through your bangs or over your shoulder, hoping for a smile, wink, or even to walk up to you and start the most idiotic conversation, even if it's about the weather. Then there's marriage. A bent knee can make a man nervous, shake, and hope for an embarrassing answer. It's always a tell-tale sign when they hear a gasp to the question before they can even ask it. Then here comes the ugly cry, and yes, they have been waiting for it, still on their knee.

The final big step in a couple's life is a bouncy baby girl or boy, or a set of twins if they're lucky. Once that occurs, the hard work of maintaining a happy home with healthy, educated children and keeping your relationship spicy by any means necessary, including remembering the fleeting feeling you had the day you saw "the one" in line at the cafeteria or the movie line, begins.

It means something different to the Islanders. It all boils down to how quickly you can dip and doge.

The Run is a long-standing tradition. It all started with two females and an argument over one male. He wasn't anything special like he could speak two languages or cook with his eyes closed, he was far from that. He owned the best land near the lake with the best view. The two females were always competing to see who could make the best bread, work the land he owned, catch a fish with their hands, and be the best of the two of them. The male found it amusing and was not as flattered as other Islanders expected; even the females vying for him became frustrated. They would chant and yell at whoever they chose. He, nevertheless, did not. He loved being the center of attention between these two beautiful women.

A group of elders watched this and were speechless. They expected him to be the man that the women saw him be. He laughed in their faces and told the elders, *"Let them figure it out. And until they do, I will benefit from it."* That was not the response they wanted. It was disrespectful not only to the women but also to them as those whom Islanders looked to for answers. However, they were ideal husbands for their wives, and they were proud of them. So, they banded together and decided for him, all of them.

Unbeknownst to the man who was asleep in his bed. The elders barged inside his home. With a crash of the door, two men grab the man and drag him outside and through the heart of the still-growing town.

Fighting back, he digs his bare feet into the dirt and yanks backward, attempting to break free. He can't because the men's skin-twisting grips pinch and burn his skin. The Islanders heard his screams but did not come to his aid. Instead, they extinguished their lanterns and shut their doors and windows. Others stand on their porches or in front of their houses, then turn their backs on him in shame, shunning him for good. He's stunned and speechless. Eventually, he gives up.

With a hunch in his back, he dips down like dew on a leaf in the morning as his arms and legs especially his ankles, are tightly double-knotted to two tall, thin pine trees. The two women walk around the group of elders and stand one by his arms, the other at his feet.

Slowly raising his head, the bound man gazes into the darkness of the woods listening to the woods speak, when he sees a tall figure come into his blurry view. He is stepping carefully and slowly on twigs in anticipation, wearing a brown sack as a hood, sweating, and the fingers on his right-hand tremble with excitement. The gap in the hood is small enough for him to see through as the moonlight illuminates his beady little eyes. The women and elders saw a slight smile rising beneath the sack.

The bound man pisses himself as he watches the man from the darkness rub his thumb on the rim of a large axe, and his blood coats it. Enjoying the fear of the bound man, the man from the darkness brings his thumb to his mouth and sucks his blood through the sack, leaving a blood stain on it as he draws the letter X on the bound man's forehead.

There is no way to make this a beautiful death because this is a sacrifice. The bound man never had the chance to scream or beg for his life. He destroyed the lives of two women, and no one knows if they would have survived. He ruined any other opportunities for another marriage. With each slice, the bound man bounces at each hack. The elders whisper, watch, and smile. The two women stood bathing in the man's blood. The one by his arm licks his arm and then traces the blood from his fingertips on her lips as if it were gloss. The other woman by his feet is giddy as his feet rip from his body, and she takes a chunk of flesh, letting his tendons and flesh squish between her teeth.

Not only were pieces of the man given to the women, but his land was their parting gift, like "till death do you part," after the elders tied a single blue ribbon on each of their fingers. Married to the dead man, the women never had chil-dren but were happy as larks. Every morning they would have tea, eat homemade bread, and blow kisses at the mantel, where the bound man's bones sat like trophies.

Ultimately, the elders were pleased to see how well the women performed. From that day forward, a new marriage law was implemented and is still in effect.

The Run.

When most celebrate Thanksgiving, Christmas, and New Year's separately, Pine Island doesn't acknowledge them. They mock it. But the Run has evolved, becoming more entertaining and enjoyable for the entire community instead of the taste of blood and slabs of flesh. It's become a way of life. At the center of attention are the singles, starting at age eighteen. All their favorite foods for one large celebration for many silent marriages.

Savoy ribs smothered in BBQ sauce with seasonings grown on the island like thyme, rosemary, and sage. The buttermilk biscuits, which are set aside for an extra three days to get that extra fluff in the dough, and the butter churned by hand for two nights straight. Lastly, they are tied in a large plastic bag inside a brown sack to represent the man in the sack mask and weighted down on the bank of the lake for freshness and taste.

The main road is slick with something that looks shiny, shimmering like a mirror from the yellow and LED lights that wrap around the pine trees on the side. Hanging from the branches and beginning to weigh them down are rotting candy canes with black spots, long braids with split ends, and pictures of the single islander with their faces scratched out. The island children's drawings on the grocery store windows show graves with hands reaching out and screaming fires, while others are of body parts with happy faces while other have pretty bows in their hair.

In the distance, single female Islanders wear long, flowing blue dresses, listening to their mothers, fathers, and siblings as they point and look at the wooded area in front of them. Swaying and moving, they practice the dodges and leaps they will make toward the chained men.

To relieve the burden of dating for the young women and men of the island, the elders, along with their families and community, assist them in making a simple and interesting choice without taking away everything. And to avoid any further deaths at the hands of the man in the brown sack, as he is now known.

The Islanders congregate on the benches and set up for the show, bringing snacks to pass down the line. They watch and prepare as the council, composed of the descendants of the elder who devised the tradition, place silver boxes in areas of the woods directly adjacent to the males chained to trees.

The men are chained, some sitting and standing, moving, clinging to their chains as they wear tight tan trousers, white-wing tip collar shirts, and bare feet. A man in black stands on the pavement, and stares down the line of the young women. With a sly smile, the man slowly steps out of the way, dragging his long, carved wooden walking stick. Anxious and ready, the women are being held back by their families as their eyes dart around and end on the man they want to be their husband. Provided they pick the correct key. The man in black taps his walking stick twice on the pavement, and the young women dash into the woods.

The goal is to retrieve a small silver box hidden in the brushes of fallen limbs, in cradling tree branches, and in the open on the ground. Each box contains a key. Once they have the key, they run, elbowing, and pushing each other out of the way to their dream husband. They insert it into the lock of one of the males chained to the tree. If the lock opens, he will be free, and they will marry. If not, then they move on to the next man.

Levi enters the crowd and laughs excitedly as a group of girls collide. He laughs and claps. Marshall Spence slaps Levi on the back of the shoulder.

"Passing again this year, Levi?"

Levi's glee fades when he sees Marshall Spence standing to his right.

"I would have thought you would be out there. Hoping to be unlocked."

"I'm not ready. Maybe next year."

"Well, it's been eighteen years. Don't you think you oughta get back out there and see who wants ya?"

"I would, but I have a feeling everyone will be after Isaiah this year. Like you said."

Isaiah grins as three girls struggle to insert their keys into his lock. He makes a celebrity-like wave. The girls and crowd applaud him as a mother calls out to her daughter, motioning for her to circle the tree, a father acts out a boxing match in the hopes that his daughter will pick up on the cues and use them. A small group of children pretend to be like the people in the woods, playing like the little boy is chained to a chair by a rope with little girls swatting and laughing at each other. This year is war, and the Islanders love every minute of it.

"I agree with you. I think this year would have been a bad year for you. I mean the pickens is becoming so small, I'm afraid you'll be a spinster of a man sooner than you think."

"Oh, I don't know about that. Don't you have a sister who has never participated in The Run yet?"

"She's seventeen," Marshall Spence says, anger building in his voice.

"Of age is age as the Elders call The Run. Most of the girls out there are fifteen and older. It seems to be me her time is dwindling. Right, Marshall." Levi says as he steps away, leaving the Marshall alone and scowling.

A smirk spreads across Levi's face as he walks toward Sadie's. Then he turns one last time to look at Marshall

Spence before entering the crowd of Islanders. The comment bothers Marshall Spence, but he shakes it off and moves toward a makeshift restroom. Stepping up, he grabs the bull-horn from one of his deputies.

"Well, it's that time of year as you can see," Marshall Spence motions to the woods. "This is the time of year, when we all come together and celebrate. We celebrate not only our traditions. But ourselves and each other. Which are so impor-tant to our way of living."

He pauses and looks down at his wife, Marla, who is at least twenty-five years his senior and has completely silver hair, wrinkles upon wrinkles, and what appears to be a small hump forming in her back, causing it to curve slightly. She is holding a small child of four, and she is the mother many adult children, some of whom are the same age as Marshall Spence. And older.

"I remember this night many years ago. I was searching for my heart. My better half. As we all know, being passed over is never fun, but that's what was happening. I felt empty. Then I heard a click."

The Islanders cheer, applaud while whooping and hollering as he pauses for dramatic effect. He loves the effect he has.

"Just when I thought all was lost, I looked up and saw my beautiful wife, Margo." He covers the mouthpiece, his eyes close, and his voice lowers. "To be honest, I don't know who was more nervous. My heart wanted to burst out of my chest, and her knees were about to give out as she began to fall. I was the one to catch her. Me. And I knew I was the luckiest man when I looked into her eyes. And now we have a small but brave little boy. We are truly blessed."

The audience applauds. Teenagers scream. Couples as young as nineteen, each with two children in their arms listen, older couples move closer together, and a man in his nineties shakes as his twenty-year-old wife places her hand over his, preventing his cane from trembling.

Excitedly, Marshall Spence yells, "And one on the way!"

The audience erupts. Marshall Spence gives the bullhorn to another I slander as he leaves the small podium and joins the crowd. He kisses Margo, deep and hard. He touches her stomach and has his other arm around her shoulders to hold her in place as she shakes from old age. Tre always thought Margo's adult children were odd even when they were teens. The reminded her like the Walton Family on acid.

"Everything is worthwhile. Bless our forefathers!" Marshall Spence screams.

Levi enters Sadie's Bar. The cheers and yells of the Islanders fade as the door shuts. Rob stands behind the counter, looking out the window as he wipes the inner rims of glasses and places them back on the rack for future use.

Levi leans against the counter, and Ron automatically pours a beer.

"Good evening, Rob."

"Levi. Happy Shredding."

"I don't know about that. It looks like it's one of those nights."

"Anything is possible, even for you."

Levi takes a large swig of his beer. Finishing his swallow, he takes a few seconds and points at Rob.

"Funny."

"Things happen for a reason."

Rob points to the back of the bar, where Levi notices Tre sitting with an empty shot glass, looking down at all the files she's still assembling and possibly a little drunk. Rob passes him another beer. Without looking, Levi picks it up and walks over.

As the females rush toward the silver boxes lying on the ground, resting in the branches, and hidden in the pine straw that has fallen while they wait, the woods simmer with flashes of blue. They open the silver boxes as quickly as they can to retrieve the rusty, long skeleton keys that are inside. They start running like a tornado to the chained men against the tree trunks. The Islanders cheer them on as they gaze in awe and excitement.

Sitting in the same booth, Tre and Levi cannot contain their laughter as they talk about old times.

"Do you remember when we tried to build a treehouse out of pine straw?" Levi asks.

Levi's laughter conveys his message effectively. Tre nearly spits her third beer all over the table and herself.

"Oh, my goodness. I had forgotten about it," Tre replies. She straightens her back and mocks Levi's voice. "This is how I'm going to build our house," you said, pulling out the duct tape and tying them together."

"Did I not sound like that?"

"You're right. You sounded much worse."

The first male is unlocked. He is thin and bony, like a skeleton with a long, jagged scar on the right side of his face, the worst hidden beneath his wiry black beard. He towers over the small-framed girl once he stands, with one arm significantly shorter than the other. They exchange a small kiss before her parents rush up to greet him, as do his parents to her. Both sets of parents shake hands and embrace each other, overjoyed that someone wanted their unusually shaped children. The new couple is unsure of their reaction. They barely exchange glances because they know they will have grandchildren sooner rather than later, preferably within a year.

A six-foot female with long blonde braids unlocks a short male; he's five feet tall. Thrilled, she picks him up like a ragdoll and cuddles him.

Another girl with brown mousy hair stands in the crowd, waving wildly to her parents, while her male's face is snarky and annoyed—not just by the girl he ended up with, but also by the smell to his left. So much for a tailwind on this run. The smell has been following him and finally knows why. He looks at a slender redhead who just unlocked a dirty and smelly fisherman, he didn't want to be with her because she smells like sour milk.

Tre and Levi look out the window as Islanders pass by.

"I remember The Run being fun when we were kids."

"We were eighteen years old and stupid."

"I understand, but we knew what we wanted."

Tre swallows her second-to-last sip of beer.

"I didn't know what I wanted." Tre says.

"Oh, come on. Yes, you did."

"No, I didn't. I didn't want to be the same as the rest. Well, you know," Tre nudges her head. Towards the window at the Islanders. "Plus, I felt trapped, and the idea of being weighed down by a marriage I never wanted and a family I wasn't ready to have? Thank you, but no."

Levi drums his fingers. He is offended by what she said and takes the conversation to a more serious turn, which Tre isn't ready for.

"You felt suffocated with me."

"No. I was never—I just wanted something different."

"You mean not me."

Tre looks at Levi as he blinks repeatedly questioning everything he hears. She reaches for his hand. But he lifts it from the table and places it on his lap. Interested in hearing what Tre has to say, he leans back. But Tre puts her foot in her mouth.

"I never wanted to be like my mother, trapped here on the island. I don't want you to hate me. But I just saw something other than a wife and mother inside me. I was never going to be who you wanted. But believe me I knew; knew you were going to be the most amazing husband and father. You deserved so much more. It just wasn't for me. Still isn't."

"We had so many things we wanted to do together. Did it all change when you unlocked me?"

"Before the click I was dreaming of a life like my mother's. But when I turned the lock, and you stood up. Then everything—everything became real."

"And you hated the thought."

"I hated Pine Island. Not you. I could never hate you."

He takes her hands into his, pushes her hair off her shoulder, and looks at her with a smile. It's been a long time since he has been this close to his fiancé as far as he is concerned.

"I have never felt like this for anyone. The moment I saw you, it all came back. I can't even be in The Run because I have always waited for you to come back. And here you are."

"I'm not here for your redemption. Or the games all of you play."

"I don't play games."

"Oh, yeah?"

Tre pulls a red pen from her bag and tears a small piece of paper from her legal notepad. She scribbles her name and Levi's in red ink on the slip. He sighs and shakes his head.

"You know red pens aren't allowed on the island."

"Why? Because some old assholes said it's not allowed?"

"Tradition says it calls death upon anything etched with it."

"Please, half the traditions are bullshit. They have changed so much that they have grown ridiculous."

After a few seconds, Tre puckers her lips and blows out hot air, moving the edge of the napkin under her beer. She curls her upper back as she grabs her chest. Levi notices.

"Tre? Are you all, right?"

Tre stares at him. Her eyes roll in the back of her head, and her hand drops from her chest. She collapses backward and goes limp, passed out. With a terrifying look, Levi pulls her body close. He searches for her pulse. He looks at the bar and sees Rob is no longer there. Levi's hand drifts down and grazes her breast. She wakes up and pushes him away.

"Watch it."

"Tre? I thought?"

"Still gullible."

"Jesus, Tre."

She walks to the restroom laughing. To mock Levi, she did a half-circle and grabbed her chest once more. As she walks around the corner, he rolls his eyes. As he prepares to take another sip of his beer, he notices some commotion outside as The Run continues. Curious, he stands and makes his way outside to see what is happening.

CHAPTER 16

RED IS THE COLOR OF DEATH

IT DOESN'T MATTER what a child is told or taught. They will always believe it. From the jolly man in red, the bunny with a bag, and even the boogeyman in the closet or under the bed, children rely on the honesty of their parents. Tre knew through her parents how her life was supposed to be, and she accepted it. She wanted it. But like a clock bleeding, the droplets became so loud when she unlocked Levi. Everything began to drown her. And she had to get out. Looking over the mouth's ripples as she made her way to the mainland, everything dissipated, and the cloud she was in floated away. The moment sunlight warmed her skin, it soaked it up because she had been in the dark for so long.

With a push, Tre closes the bathroom door. She rests her head against it and takes a long, deep breath. Now she's feeling she might have the heart attack she just faked. Levi has always affected her, from the first time they held hands as babies, played in the sandbox her father made, danced in the rain when they were twelve, and told each other secrets and dreamed of a life together at sixteen. She remembers him kissing the inside of her palm since they were not allowed to kiss until marriage. She also remembers the second Levi was unlocked everything instantly faded away. She loved him, but not the way he treated her. The veil of the island lifted, and the reality of their shelter and the isolated world—their private island—opened her eyes.

She reaches into her pocket for the slip of paper with her and Levi's names written on it. She takes it out. Their names have vanished. She jumps off the door, flipping the small piece of paper back and forth. It's a clean yellow piece with blue lines on it. She knows that she jotted their names down. She turns her other pockets inside out and discovers nothing except lint.

A small drop of sweat formed on her brow. She doesn't believe in customs. She is not a believer in curses. She is skeptical of everything that occurs on this island. It has to be a trick. Maybe she had another paper; after all, she's so inebriated that anything is possible. Even so, she becomes nervous.

She dashes over to the toilet, drops the paper, and flushes it. She slams the lid shut. She sits on it, her head in her hands, listening to the water filter out and the new water come in. She bursts out laughing.

"You're losing it, Tre."

As she gets up, the toilet lid wobbles. She splashes water on her face, and when she looks in the mirror, she sees a smiley face with devil horns in place of the mirror. She lowers her head, closes her eyes, and vigorously rubs them. She leans against the sink and returns her gaze to the smiley face.

"At least one of us is happy."

She taps the smiley face on the brow before turning and walking away. The toilet starts bubbling. Water slowly streams through the crack between the lid and seat and over the edge. The water streaks run clear, gathering at the base of the toilet. Soon it becomes light pink. The more water, the more the pink darkens and becomes red like the ink on the paper Tre flushed. As the water darkens and pushes upward on the lid, it lifts and drops harder. The water is now thicker and darker than the ink of a red pen. It's blood.

Tre mulls over what she's going to say to Levi as she pushes her sleeves up and walks down the hallway. She comes around the corner to face him. He's not there. She stops and purses her lips. She walks over to the table to get her files and bag when she hears a commotion outside. She looks around the bar for Rob, but he isn't there. She leaves the files on the booth's table and walks over to the door, assuming he's outside.

She looks out the stained-glass window. She can see figures forming a growing circle in the haze. Perhaps a gang. She walks out, pushing the door open.

The Islanders have gathered a sizable crowd. Some stand back and watch as they talk and cheer amongst themselves. They all have big, bright smiles. Someone important must have unlocked Isaiah, the new golden child. Maybe a member of the council's daughter was the lucky one. What a beautiful wedding that will be.

Tre approaches a group of mothers who are conversing. They'd be the ones to figure out who's behind the gossip. Of course, they notice her and hurry away. Tre knew it was a bad idea, but she had no choice but to try. Where's Ollie when you need him? The way he has been welcomed by the Islanders; Tre assumes they would spill their life stories. The problem is would he even ask without her telling him too. Doubtful.

Still unable to see a thing, Tre hoists herself up with the help of a pole on the grocery store's porch. Islanders are gathered in the middle of the main road. It looks like they are protecting something. Tre balances herself on the rail as she stretches onto her tiptoes.

She skims the tops of their head, hoping to find an opening. She tries to pinpoint Levi, Ollie, or Marshall Spence. Unfortunately, she can't. Then she stops and almost falls off the rail, in shock. Mr. and Mrs. Morel rush out. As they hold onto each other, they walk right past her, never looking at her as the crowd follows. Colby Morel lifts his head and turns it toward her.

Losing her balance, she drops and lands in the arms of Colby Morel. His eyes are vacant. His touch is cold, his face is bluish, and he is skeletal due to significant weight loss. He smiles at her as he tightens his grip around the back of her neck, pulling her hair and skin between his long and slender fingers. He brings her closer to his dry and cracked lips. She tries to back away, but he is much stronger than he appears.

In a whispering voice, he says, "Darkness has no sound until it's given. Are you that someone, Theresa?" He licks her lobe with his white tongue.

She jerks back, only to find herself in Levi's arms, his sparkling eyes fixed on her. And Colby is across the main road, leering at her as his mother places a blanket around his shoulders as his father happily shakes hands with the council. A long stream of drool spills from Colby's mouth as he stares at her and brings his balled-up hand in front of him. Opening his hand, Colby shows a bundle of her hair from the back of her neck and blows it away. He begins hysterically laughing.

"Isn't it great, Tre? Colby is back."

Astonished, Tre watches Levi falls in line with the rest of the crowd as they all begin walking down the main road, singing and cheering. Mesmerized, she listens to the Islanders sing and cheer as they descend the main road. She realizes she is stepping on a tangle of chains. Looking down, Tre pushes them with her shoe. When she looks back up, they are gone.

Alone and perplexed, she freezes mid-step, letting her foot dangle in the air just inches above the ground. She has felt this sensation before. Slowly, she sets her foot onto the ground. The uncomfortable and undeniable rush of electricity charges and raises the hair on your arms as you look across a bedroom to see a closet door slightly ajar. Ever so slightly, but enough to allow the monster inside to escape. The slow slice a razor makes against peachy-subtle skin as its blood seeps out and onto the white floor, blemishing it. The creature from under the bed, a hand that creeps over the edge of the bed to a sleeping child, stealing them away forever into a dark world filled with screams and howls. Tre knows someone is watching her, waiting for her to make a mistake.

Tre isn't carrying her weapon. She feels the sensation growing stronger, almost like it's wrapping its arms around her body like an ice blanket. She places her foot carefully, never turning around as she makes a fist, and is prepared to defend herself if necessary. She swings around, counting her breaths to three. She comes to a halt in shock. She's staring at herself.

Tre, dressed in a long white nightgown, watches herself giggle as if someone unseen has told her a funny joke. Tre, unable to move, observes herself turn and waves to her to follow. Did Tre drink too much? What is Rob serving at the bar? Her lookalike turns and waves to Tre before running into the woods. Automatically, Tre takes off after her.

The mist forming on the ground makes the run after herself feel ghostly and moribund. The other Tre finds the chase fun and giggles as she stops and looks back behind her, waiting for Tre to catch up. Tre steps through the small patch of darkness into the inner part of the woods.

With a grin of excitement on her face, Tre in white snickering and stops for a second, listening to Tre as she tries to catch up, breaking twigs and crunching leaves below her feet. In love with the chase, the Tre in white lets the mist surround her like a guide to the other side of the woods.

For Tre, being chased by herself is the best way to wake up. Tre listens as the other Tre's laughter echoes around her as she dashes away. Tre tries to catch up, but the other Tre runs faster. As she dips to avoid falling tree limbs, she never looks

STACEY L. PIERSON

back. She leaps over the downed trees as they dry out and soak into the ground as if they are returning home. Tre continues to imitate the other Tre's every move.

Tre is unaware that they are running in a circle until she passes the opening a fourth time. Suddenly, the other Tre vanishes before her eyes as the mist splits in half.

Tre comes to a halt. She can't believe what she's just witnessed. A woman, her other self, has just vanished. She blinks and twirls slowly, trying to remember which way she went. Then she hears sticks being hit in the distance. She hears trees cracking all around her as if they are about to fall to the ground. They never do, however.

Tre looks over her shoulder in time to see the other Tre rushes at her. The other Tre takes her face with her cold and withering hands. The other Tre looks at her in the eyes as she leans in, puckering her lips as she hums *Frère Jacques* in a soft voice. Underneath is a hoarse, almost toneless chant and more sinister singing, off by a second per word. Unknowingly, the ever-growing grass Tre is standing on begins to stretch, inching its way toward her legs. The other Tre's mouth begins to pry open, widening and dislocating her jaw. Suddenly, Tre gets hit from the side, knocking her out of the way. The other Tre watches, her body hovering off the ground. Her eyes turn hollow as her hums turn to a screech that emanates from her evaporating body. Once Tre breaks free from the hypnotic pull, she becomes aware of the world around her. Two bright lights surround her.

The continuous rotation of Tre's head causes her to grab her belt as a lantern pierces her shadow. The other Tre tries to break through, trying to touch her. But the light moved in front of her a second before. Tre feels like a solid wall has appeared next to her. She looks out of the corner of her eye.

She is relieved. It's Finkle. He stays close to her as he tries to keep the other Tre away while keeping them in the light.

A rotten hand appears and tries to use its petrified fingernail to scratch at them. With an echoing shrill, the other Tre lunges, and her smell is of bleach and decay. Her skin silts with every touch of the lanterns as Finkle moves them around. Giving up but not in, the other Tre steps back into the darkness with a sad cry. Not willing to answer any questions at that point, Finkle and Tre take off running as the moonlight flutters through the treetops and branches. The other Tre disappears as the lanterns bounce between Finkle and Tre. With nature and the darkness calming around them, Finkle hands Tre a lantern.

Their feet shuffle through the dead leaves and pine straw accumulates in their laces as they charge through the woods. The wind whistles as loud as a train as it follows them, destroying and sawing through thin weak trees and causing loose dirt to swirl in the air like a tornado. Finkle is pointing a few steps ahead.

"There's an opening up ahead," Finkle yells at Tre. She looks back for a split second and notices the darkness grows to keep the lantern's light from breaking through. She comes to a halt.

"Come on," Finkle screams.

Tre raises the lantern as Finkle disappears in front of her. She leans forward, allowing the lantern to light her path as she looks ahead. Long and dimming in the shadow cast by the lantern's brightness, the trees to her sides move and try to grab her by their branches gradually turn into human hands..
"Jacob?"

Finkle's boot slams into the wet ground, leaving ridged sole prints before the soil breathes them in. He stammers and dodges his way out of the woods, landing on his side as he slides out through the opening and onto a paved road under a streetlight. While resting on his knees, he notices he is alone.

His heartbeat quickens, and he exclaims, "Tre? Tre?"

His boot tips scratch the pavement as he twists them. Scared and shaking, he holds his lantern up.

"Are you there, Tre?"

He feels like he's taken a step back in time. He has always been the faster runner between him and Tre. But one thing he knows she has always shown forty-nine seconds behind him. Tre is trailing Finkle with her lantern, which bobs and flies back and forth as she tries to catch up. She notices that the path is no longer a path, the trail is no longer a trail, and the closing is no longer what it was when they were children.

The opening to the playground or "their place" as they refer to it, is a masterfully macabre den where hunts and callings rather than games like hide-and-seek and Marco Polo. It is perilous. Because the brass eye knows what it sees, everything seems strange and deceiving. Nakedness and the shallowness with which the light breathes down on them as they let the wind cover them with loose petals of flowers they never saw. But the aroma is strong.

Finkle dips his head under the hanging pines faster than expected, he pushes for his collar down and then fixes the wild strands of his hair. He steps into further into the light and slowly leans over, exhaling a sigh of relief. Even with the sobering alcohol swirling around his veins, he has no idea Tre wasn't right behind him.

From Tre's eyesight, she watches as Finkle's lantern suddenly disappears as he exits the woods before her. She picks up speed as slowing and shaking with the thunder rolls behind her.

Tre emerges from the drooping branches and slips her arm into the warmth of the streetlight, and freezes. She is half-faint and frantic. Whispers tickle her earlobes, hot air brushes her neck, and icy pinpoints like fingers walking down her arm fall like waking goosebumps. The hair on her arm stands up straight in fear.

Finkle's brows raise as he watches fear dance around them. Tre darts her gaze toward him. Her cheeks sink, and her breathing becomes erratic. He extends his hand to her. Her fingertips are starting to wrinkle as if they've been in a cold bowl of ice water, and her nails are chipping. Paleness tints her skin and causes her to shake.

The whispers sing sinister carols with lyrics she doesn't understand. As Finkle moves closer, loose gravel scratches the pavement beneath his boots. Half of her gradually fades into the darkness and grays. Finkle freezes in place. Barely an inch away from her hand, the heat on her neck draws him closer. A puff of white smoke parts between Tre's lips; her hair, hidden in the darkness, blows from the heavy sigh. Darkness sighs.

As Tre stares at Finkle, a cloudy tear forms in her graying eye. She mouths, *I love you* through her dry, peeling-like-bark lips. The words smacked Finkle in the chest like a stake. He will not let her go. He already lost her, and he will not again. Finkle braces himself against the pavement and wraps his hand around hers as darkness descends and swallows the light. Frost encircles their hands. Tre's gaze moves swiftly from Finkle as he sees the whites of her eyes and her face freezes. As she fades into the darkness, Finkle jerks her toward him.

He yanks with everything he has. He buckles at the knees, lands on sharp-edged small rocks, and rears backward as the frost turns to ice and covers his arm. As the darkness absorbs Tre, he leans further back. Shot like a slingshot, Tre lands in Finkle's arms. He clings to her. She's trembling uncontrollably. He grabs her face and looks her in the eyes. Tre's eyes are glassy, the peeling skin on her lips are white and dead, and her cheeks become more sunken than they were before. The longer she stays on Pine Island, the more she will fade away.

Trembling, Tre asks, "Was that me?"

"Now you see why I'm always drunk."

CHAPTER 17
IT'S IN THE BLOOD

THERE ARE MANY NAMES—SPECTER, phantom, shadow, wraith, lookalike—but many know them as doppelgangers. But how did they come about? No one knows. And no one knows what they think about being branded without being asked. There is no doubt that they are special and as captivating as sirens.

When Lilibeth watched her mother in labor in the 1800s, she held her fabric doll with a white face and red hair. Besides her little brother Stanley, a two-year-old, blonde haired, small-framed boy with piercing blue eyes, she sat strapped to a chair, looking nervous. He kept leaning and looking around the corner, interested in what was happening. Lilibeth ruffles his curly hair at the top of his head. They laugh. Stanley reaches for the doll with his long midnight black claws. Waring of the claw tips, Lilibeth teases him by repeatedly by bringing it to and from his face. She makes him close his eyes as she tickles his nose with the doll's hair. Suddenly, their mother's screams grew louder.

The midwife, sweaty and staring at the woman in labor, she urges her to push inside the bedroom. The pain is excruciating, and the child inside rolls around in her stomach before coming out. In the back, the father walks back and forth, his fingers running through his long, brown, and wiry beard. He's hesitant to look but desires to be present for his wife. The child inside stretches and pushes on her flesh as if it were rubber. She grits her teeth.

"Encore une poussée et le bébé sera là. (One more push and the baby will be here,)" the midwife yells.

"Non, je ne peux pas. Je ne peux pas. (No, I can't. I can't.)"

The woman in labor's head falls back, weeping and exhausted. As the woman rises from the bed and the baby forces itself out, the midwife turns to face the woman in labor husband. Her skin rips, and tears stream down her hot red cheeks. She clutches the bed's edges in agony and screams at the top of her lungs.

Blood drenched the midwife as she collected more and more of the now-red-white sheet in her hands. The woman in labor immediately recoils and the midwife's face turns pale as the child is born and rests in her arms. As she looks the baby doesn't coo. Instead, a small roar escapes the baby's lips.

The mother's body is relaxed. She is free of the intense and violent pressure she was experiencing. The midwife looks at her while she is still bleeding.

"Est-ce que mon bébé est d'accord? Pourquoi n'ai-je pas entendu un cri? (Is my baby all right? Why haven't I heard a cry?)"

The husband takes a step forward. He looks at the child. Without warning, he starts to panic as he whimpers and talks to himself. His wife was weak and pale, barely able to speak or breathe. She lowered her gaze to the midwife. That's when she sees her brand-new baby for the first time.

A paw raises through the flickering lantern and candle flames, not a hand with five fingers, a palm ready to wrap around their mother's fingers. Tiny claws and pinkish pads move and wrinkle, stretching and feeling the new world's air. The midwife begins to shake. She is too terrified to move or gasp because this isn't the first time, she and her family have witnessed an unusual birth in this small town.

"Le Seigneur nous a maudits une fois de plus ma femme. ("The lord has cursed us once more my wife.)"

"Nous le laisserons dans les bois pour que la nature sauvage le prenne. Nous allons réessayer. (We shall leave it in the woods for the wildness to take it. We shall try again.")"

"Non. Nous - ne pouvons pas... (No. We - can't...")"

"À cause de toi, ma postérité est damnée pour ta fréquentation avec le diable dans les bois. Je ne vous dénoncerai pas tout de suite. Je veux qu'un autre enfant porte mon nom. Un fils. Ou vous brûlerez comme les autres membres de votre coven l'ont fait. (Because of you, my seed is damned for your consorting with the devil in the woods. I shall not turn you in just yet. I want another child to bear my name. A son. Or you will burn like the others in your coven did.)"

The husband walks out, pausing to look at Stanley, who chuckles. With a smile, Stanley reaches his claws out and wants to be picked up. The mother is crying mumbling something no one can understand as she tries to get out of bed. Swallowing hard, his father reluctantly picks him up. When Stanley tries to touch his father's face with his claws, it is pushed away. The father turns to the midwife.

"Apportez-le et ne me perdez pas de vue. (Bring it and do not lose sight of me.)"

As the midwife gathers the baby, she stands to leave. The mother stops her.

"Sage-femme! (Midwife!)"

The midwife never says anything but look back at the mother with tears streaming down her face. But still, she dashes out the open front door to catch up with the master of the house and Stanley as they make their way through the dark woods. A gust of wind blows, and Lilibeth looks out as Stanley waves with the doll. She looks down at her hands and notices that it has vanished. The mother weakened falls back onto her back, staring at the water damaged spot on the ceiling, she mouths words. Lilibeth starts crying and runs to her mother, whose eyes are open and cloudy due to blood loss. Lilibeth jolts her. But nothing happens.

"Maman? Maman? ("Mama? Mama?)"

Her mother is dead. Her father has left her. The midwife followed. And her little brother has been taken along with her new baby sibling. The only comfort Lilibeth has is her knees, which she draws into her chest while sitting in the corner.

Stanley and the newborn are sitting in the dark. He leans over and grabs the red sheets as he listens to the night sounds of frogs, crickets, and the caws of birds he can't see above. A rustle in the bushes catches his attention. A ball rolls across the grass, hitting small bumps before stopping as it bounces off his bare foot. With his big blue eyes, she watches as a footprint appears and begins to walk toward him. He's not afraid or nervous. He remains there and observes.

The footprints bare down in the soil, leaving creases, and each toe grows longer and narrower with each step. As it gets closer to Stanley and the baby, a hazy shadow comes into focus, becoming more solid. Stanley takes a position in front of the infant. He digs his heels deep as his toes lengthen and pierce the ground, lowering his chin to his chest. He snaps his wrist beside him to reveal his claws, which are darkening and becoming sharper, while his eyes shimmer in gold and yellow hues. Deep within his gut, a growl begins to erupt, shaking his chest as his heart beats, pushing the flesh on his chest.

It emerges from a dark shadow.

Her shadow drops off and slinks back toward the darkness, forming towering figures. She stops a foot away. Her skin is flawless. The moonlight grazes her face as the darkness seeps through the branches where her skin is scaly and prickly, with a snake-shaped eyes and a thin edge to her mouth. The baby cries, and Stanley is ready to strike. She laughs.

"Well now, little one. You are a fighter. I like that."

She pinches Stanley's nose to keep it from stretching outward. When she touches him, he relaxes. As she gets down on one knee and takes his hands, he gradually transforms into the little boy from before. She inspects his claws.

"You should be proud of who and what you are. Your grandfather would be. He was like you. Now you are like him, inquisitive and brave to the core." Stanley looks at her with a smile as she reveals her long, reptile-like tail. It curls around her and grazes her long black hair that's hugging her face.

She casts a glance behind him. In the sheet, the baby is moving. She never let's go of his hands as they turn to look after the baby. Stanley tightens his claws around her wrists as a warning. She picks up on the hint.

"I would never hurt family," she tells him as her tail whips and sways.

Stanley lets her examine the baby, but with only one hand. The baby laughs and coos. As the baby grabs and wraps its paws around the woman's finger, she holds her human hand out into the air so Stanley is comfortable.

"She's amazing. How about we call her Emme? After your great-great-grandmother. She would be proud."

The woman picks up Emme. As she stands up, she looks at Stanley. "You are a very brave little boy and both of you will grow to be a miracle for our people. Leaders as some would say. We are family. I am Sabine. Your and Emme's humble servant. Until the night disappears."

Sabine, Stanley, and Emme walk into the darkness and vanish.

After reaching young adulthood, Stanley and Emme become more interested in the world and its inhabitants, especially those who are attractive and single. But as they walk down the small road in the middle of town they watch adults flee in fear, and parents yank their children from their games, closing their doors or hiding.. A young man stands on his cabin's porch, staring at Emme. He has feelings for her. Despite his smile, he was dragged inside by the collar of his deep tan shirt before any words were said. The young man's father fires eye daggers at Emme as he slams the door. Dropping her hand, she shakes her head and folds her arms.

"I still don't understand why people hide from us. Especially when we were children."

"We were children. Plus, we remind them of those who have passed."

"I know, I know, we aren't supposed to exist, blah, blah, blah. It's not fair."

Stanley senses Emme's growing rage and can hear the black spiky fur breaking through her skin and strong enough to break through her clothes. He takes her hand in his.

"We are meant for greatness. And we exist because well, it was written in the dark, as Sabine says. Be happy."

"Happy. You want me to be happy. I can't even like someone without their father or mother taking them away from me."

"Emme, there's more to life than love. It's overrated. Besides, you have me, and I have you. Isn't that enough? "

"No. It's not. I want more. I want children one day."

They come to a halt. Stanley is staring at her. He's never heard her talk about or even mention children. He's at a loss for words.

"What?" Stanley asks.

"Nothing."

"Don't you want to be with someone who loves you?" She looks around and notices a young woman standing on the porch, stunned. Frozen, staring, desperately trying to speak, all her mouth does is move without saying anything. She is tall, her hair in a bun beneath an off-white bonnet. "How about her?"

Emme gestures to the young lady. Going to amuse her, Stanley turns around and abruptly stops. He locks his gaze on her. A small girl of three pokes her head around the young woman's hip, holding a doll. A faceless doll with worn-out clothes and tattered red hair. A flood of memories returns.

Lilibeth grabs her doll and pulls it away from Stanley.

Lilibeth turns away from him.

Stanley is tearing one of the dolls apart with his claws while Lilibeth has a temper tantrum.

Stanley looks over his father's shoulder while being carried away from home, and Lilibeth grins at him. He waves at her with her redheaded doll, and she runs off crying to their mother.

Lilibeth shields her daughter as she stumbles backward as rushes inside her house. But the walls of her house cannot silence nor hide her for long. Like eyes blurring from staring too long, Stanley focuses his attention on Lilibeth's breathing. He can hear her heart skip a beat and her breathing becomes more rapid. Her bones tremble as she stacks things against her front door. Emme, bewildered, swung her gaze from Lilibeth's house to Stanley. She observes his claws gradually and steadily growing.

"Who is that?"

Hearing her, Stanley snaps back to reality. Taking a deep breath, he turns his attention to Emme. He acts as if nothing has happened.

"No one. Just an old friend."

"You have friends? Yeah, right. And I know you're not going to tell me."

"Come on, Sabine is waiting."

As Stanley jogs back to Lilibeth's house, the sky darkens towards the side of the house, where he stands waiting for the front door to swing open. A man in black, holding a hat and a book, steps out and turns to Lilibeth. She adjusts his collar.

"You will be great."

"I wish you could be there."

"I know, but Hope is sick and does not need to be around those healthy."

"I understand. I love you, Lilibeth."

He leans in and kisses her cheek before walking down the steps toward the church at the end of the road. He turns back and waves as he rushes away, listening to the choir begin to sing. She comes to a sudden halt mid-wave as her husband becomes part of the night. Something isn't quite right. The wind dies down, taking the chill of the night with it, and a dryness surrounds her and crawls down her throat. She sneezes. She spits blood out. She wipes the small stream from her chin as it lands on the wood in a circle. She quickly wipes it away and dashes inside.

Lilibeth walks over to the fireplace. The flame is fading. She puts another log inside and waits for it to flare up again. She grabs a frame from the mantel. The drawing depicts her father on his wedding day to the woman, now stepmother, who would later adopt and become Lilibeth's mother. In the background of the wedding picture is her grandfather, now deceased, scowling. He looks exactly like Stanley. She traces her fingers around his face when she's startled by a broom drop.

When she sees the broom, she exhales as she replaces the drawing on the mantel. She approaches and bends down. A shadow passes through the fire as her palm grasps the tip. She comes to a halt. She takes her time standing. Heavy breathing can be heard behind her, scorching her neck. Her gaze turns to Hope's room. Her bed is bare. Blankets are everywhere, the pillow is on the floor, and her red-haired doll is in pieces. But there is no sign of Hope.

"Where is my Hope?"

"She is in a better place."

"Stanley, what did you do?"

"You watched as father walked me to my death."

"I was a child."

Stanley places his hand on Lilibeth's shoulders. He drags his claws up and down her dress, spreading the wrinkles and slowly slicing the edges.

"So was I."

Stanley moves his claws to her throat and wraps them around it. He flings her around. She hits the walls, is tossed over chairs, and tries to flee, but he is too fast for her. She collides with the table. He slashes at her, and slices open her back. She screams. His growls are deep as he feels the veins in her neck extract blood, fueling his rage at the fact that she is still alive. Lilibeth was an ideal child. She was their father's favorite child. He would go to any length for her. But not Stanley. He wanted him to leave. He wanted him to vanish along with the curse he believed was on his family.

"Gaze upon me, sister. Look what I have become. What I was meant to be."

She screams as she opens her eyes. She tries to free herself from Stanley's grip. But he won't let her go. He is determined to make her realize that by failing to help him, not only did she not stop him from their father leading him to his death, but she brought him to a family. A family who would teach him his true origins because of their mother and father's choices. They adored him and respected who and what he is.

The beast has been passed down from generation to generation, affecting only children born after the first. The devil was furious to see the coven; his children were burned and drowned for loving him. He promised the townspeople that they would remember what they had done, and he bestowed black magic on his children's children. For many years, births went unnamed until a priest declared them doppelgangers because they resembled the community's pillars—their mothers' fathers.

As Lilibeth hits Stanley's hand, he pierces her skin with the tips of his sharp claws. Blood slides down her neck and gathers at her collar and cross brooch. He licks her neck as a final goodbye kiss.

"See you in hell, dear sister. Say hello to father for me."

Stanley pulls her back with a howl. Her eyes glisten, and her last breath is cut short. With strength, he places his claws on either side of her head. He effortlessly pries her skull open. Her skull shifts and cracks like an egg, and blood pours everywhere, showering Stanley as her body falls to the floor. A piece of her brain is sitting in his hands. He takes a bite. With each chew, he feels superior and enjoys Lilibeth as a pickled human. He is satisfied.

Stanley and Emme will be the last of their bloodline from now on.

CHAPTER 18

GRANDMA'S GHOST STORY

TRE GRIPS the edge of the blanket that she's wrapped up in. She looks at the color of her skin; it's bluish. She presses down lightly and the blue disappears for a second as the white or as a Sabine would say her body temperature is too low. Scared, she pulls her hand in to help it get warm. She tucks her chin into her chest as Finkle hands her a mug. She refuses.

"It will make you warm."

"I think I've had enough to drink."

Finkle urges her to take it and says, "Don't worry, it's not booze. It's hot cocoa."

Tre takes it and sniffs it. Finkle turns and plops down in the chair near the fire.

"Well, if you change your mind, you know who to ask. Hell, the first time it happened to me, I drank myself to sleep for days if not a few weeks." Finkle tilts a bottle of whiskey and says right before he takes a swig, "Fucking terrifying."

"Who was that? "

"No, not who. But what was that? What."

"What was that?"

Finkle licks his lips as if he's too nervous to tell the story. But now that it's happened to Tre, he can't lie to her anymore.

Or rather, he needs to remind her of something they have known since they were little.

"Remember that story grandma used to tell us right before we went to bed?"

Tre thinks for a few seconds, and nothing hits her.

"Yeah, I didn't either until I met him."

"Him?"

"My doppelganger."

Tre gets up and moves closer to the fire as Finkle takes another swig. He doesn't want to talk about it, but he is. She can see he's scared, frightened of anything and everything that has to do with this topic.

"Most parents tell their kids not to talk to strangers, but they never said anything like that to us. It was all because we grew up here, the sickle island where we all see each other all the time. But when it was grandma's turn to tuck us into bed. She would kiss us on the forehead, and tell us not to talk to ourselves, no matter how nice we are."

"I don't remember that."

"You will. It's like our memories are gone, taken, or switched until we see ourselves. The ones she told us not to talk to ."

The fire flickers and warms the side of Finkle's face as he begins the story where their grandma would always start off.

"She said it all began with a lie."

Outside, the darkness steps closer to the house as the wind picks up.

"A lie between families."

"Whose families?"

"Ours and the Priest's. And it became a bloodbath."

"Come. Come kiss my lips and you'll find out. You wouldn't be the first."

Holding hands, Emme turns to Stanley and together they loudly cackle which causes their accomplices to snicker.

"Enough!"

Two townsmen rush in and a long-haired bearded man named Sir, Lilibeth's father-in -law and head of the town, the right hand of the Lilibeth. The whites of Stanley's eyes shine bright as they roll to the back of his head as he listens to the breeze of whispers blowing in Sir's ear. Emme narrows her eyes as the edges of her mouth curl, growing larger with delight, and Stanley opens his mouth. A black widow spider carefully crawls out, and a bark centipede slowly inches up his throat and comes out.

"For your crime you shall perish in the depths of hell where you belong," Sir tells them.

"I welcome it." Emme snaps.

"Fear is not in our hearts, but in yours. You have murdered many children and women because they are not you. You fear change and the chance to be a higher being. But us. We welcome it and know who and what we are," Stanley preaches.

"For the murder of my dear Lilibeth…"

"I'm sure she was YOUR Lilibeth." Emme takes a deep breath in.

"My family, their family, our family…your family. You shall die," Sir shouts.

Breathing in Sir's scent, Stanley smirks, "From your scent. She was more than a dear. A lover. A mother. The whore next to you when her husband is away."

"You must ask if your daughter could very well be your sister," Emme says to Lilibeth's husband as he stands behind his Sir, his father.

Locke, Lilibeth's husband, charges at her but is stopped by strong men. He is broken and falls to his knees, loudly sobbing. Emme and Stanley laugh. This amuses them.

"As their accomplices, you are excommunicated to the islands off the mainland. Never step foot on the mainland forevermore. Your descendants are no longer welcome. Your magic is wrapped, and you will never be able to use it if you find your way back through the fog. Let the scissors snip."

Sir looks at the fair-haired child hiding behind one of the coven members with tear stains down his rosy cheeks. Sir watches as the child darts toward him but is caught by two men. As they hold him in the air, he is screaming, crawling, and trying to scratch at the Sir's eyes. The child hisses and waves his twisted tongue. Violently, Sir grabs the child by the bangs of his hair and tosses him into the arms of a weary elderly woman. She comforts the child as he struggles to bite the man.

"To end their bloodline, they must be banded as well."

"Could the blood be cleansed?" A coven member steps forward and asks.

"No."

The two siblings reach out and clasp their hands. The ground below trembles. Cracking like a shell being forcibly pried open, the ground begins to split as a hot wind begins to cause members of the coven to blister. One of the male coven members catches his hair as it falls from his head, a woman rips her shirt from her skin as her breasts bubble and boil, and a man drops to his knee and holds her pelvis as three blobs of tissue, flesh, and blood roll down his pants leg.

Emme and Stanley stare at the chaos and land their hollowing eyes on Sir. Frightened and shocked, he watches as their followers hold their palms outward, head to the sky, and stand stark naked due to their clothes burning off, a melodic song like a hum.

"It's not the dark," Stanley mouths.

"But what's in the dark," Emme finishes.

Roars in the distance slow the fire and the coven's voices silence. Scared, they search each other's eyes with no answers. The siblings' accomplices bend on their knees as the twisted tongue child screeches. Sir notices the ropes are empty. Emme and Stanley are gone. One by one the throats of those who put their hands on the siblings are sliced, their blood spilled and their bodies burned. In the ashes of their flesh, footsteps approach. There's a sinister laugh and

Emme blows Sir grabs his cheek as two cuts appear and split his cheek. The bones of his jaw peek through his hand that tries to hold his face together. His right eye turns into the back of his head as he slowly falls onto his side.

Unable to speak, he watches as Emme and Stanley saunter toward their bowing followers. . The darkness engulfs the followers, and they disappear.

Suddenly, the trembles inside the muscles in his face stop. Sir feels his face. Relieved he is released from the nightmare inflicted on him. He looks around to see his men are fine expect one. Staring without eyes, and half a tongue hanging out, Sir's heart breaks. He has lost his firstborn son.

"Father," a young man hollers as he rushes toward him.

"Zachary."

Sir wraps his arm around his son's neck and helps him stand.

"I thought I lost you.".

"I believed I was. But your brother..."

"I'm sorry, father. I betrayed you."

Sir stares. Zachary bows his head. He doesn't want to speak because of the reaction he will get. But he knows if he doesn't, the punishment will be worse.

"Emme bewitched me, and I gave in to temptation."

A young man attempts to wave at Emme as she walks through the middle of the road. His father grabs and yanks him inside their home with the collar. The door is slammed.

Sir doesn't know what to say.

"She is with child. My child."

Zachary and Emme meet in the woods. Kissing. Zachary pins her against a tree as he kisses her neck. Heavy breathing. She pulls her dress up as he takes off his suspenders .

Sir takes his son into his arms and holds him tight. Zachary keeps apologizing, but Sir reassures him he did nothing wrong as a man. But as a human.

"The darkness is within the child now. But we are now tied to her line for eternity."

"How am I to see my child?"

"When the time is right. The child will escape and be with their true family. But be warned. They will always have a tie to the island."

They look out across the water to see a fire burning bright on the island with cheers and chants. On the edge of the water line, Emme rubs her stomach and smiles.

"We will return, and darkness walked the mainland once again."

"So, we are their vessels or some shit like that?"

Finkle chugs his drink and looks at her.

"I don't know. Grandma was crazy by the time she died. She also said aliens visited her from time to time. Plus, she would be found in all areas of the island stark naked and rambling about being a bird who fell from the nest."

"Come on, there has to be something to it. She was one of the oldest people who ever lived here."

"Damn Tre, you act like she was from the golden day-no, the stone-age."

"What happened when you met yourself?"

"I was drunk. I had just returned from the mainland. I stepped off onto the dock…"

———

"And there I was."

Finkle leans and stares as he watches himself rush at him. Charging at full speed. He tries to run, but his feet become jumbled and he loses his balance.

He falls into the water. A quick, refreshing, and instantly sobering experience. He splashes around, seeing no one, not even himself.

———

"There has to be something around here about this."

"I doubt it. When grandma and mom died, dad had Sabine clean both of their rooms up. Grandmas was given to the houses around her, but mom's stuff. It was burned. In the barrels in the back."

"He burned everything?"

"Everything. Including our family pictures, especially the ones with us in them. Well, you."

Tre brings her warm fingers to her lips.

"If he did that, how come my room is the same?"

"Sabine talked him into leaving it because she believed you would come back to stay."

"Why did she do that? Another promise to mom?"

"I guess."

Finkle rubs his eyes and yawns, then says, "I gotta get some sleep. You should too. You had a hard night." He places his hand on her shoulder and grips it tight. "I'm glad you're okay, sis. I love you."

"Me too. Thank you, Finkle. I love you too."

Finkle leaves. Tre gets up and looks out the window before she lays down to sleep. If she can sleep after tonight.

On the ground, deep impressions are drawn closer. and move up the stairs. A deep-seated growl rumbles in the night. The door flies open, and Mrs. Forgeron drops her cup of tea as she screams. She tries to run up the stairs, but she is dragged down and out the front door. She is able to grab the door-frame. The darkness is too strong. She slowly begins to lose her grip, watching her finger slip off the doorframe, and is dragged out the front door. It slams. Her screams drop and rise as she is dragged down the stairs, through the night and into the woods. Mr. Forgeron never wakes, and the entire house is silent as Katie Forgeron walks down the dirt road. Back home.

CHAPTER 19
PUTTING ALL THE PIECES TOGETHER BEFORE NIGHTTIME

MARSHALL SPENCE BURSTS through the door and comes to a halt. He takes a satisfying inhale and lets out a chuckle. Tre leaps from the small sofa on which she is sleeping. Tre watches as Marshall Spence appears in her line of sight. Junior deputies rush into other parts of the house—the kitchen and dining room, and a few stomps up the stairs—on a mission. They don't want to let Marshall Spence down.

With his head held high, Marshall Spence inhales the freshness of the house but he's mire presence makes the air stale. Tre moves closer to Marshall Spence as his gaze falls on her. He has a sly grin on his face.

"Just who I am looking for."

"What is going on?" Tre inquires as she observes the junior deputy rummaging through drawers and toppling cushions from the sofa and chairs. Upstairs, she listens as the junior deputies make the sound of a herd of buffalo trampling through a field, dropping everything in their wake. Finkle rushes down the stairs, putting his plaid shirt over his white undershirt, confused, and enraged.

"What the fuck Jamieson?"

"That's Marshall Spence, Finkle. Like it's always been when we meet."

"Is that before or after you bitch about not getting it up for your croon of a wife because you keep whacking it to one of your deputies?"

Marshall Spence points his finger and furrows his brow. "You better watch your mouth, son. Or you'll find yourself on the wrong side of the island."

"That's not a threat you dick."

Tre looks around as the junior deputies start carrying out her personal items. One of them appears and hands Marshall Spence Tre's weapon. Tre goes for it. He moves it away and places his hand in front of her face. Happily, he tells her, "Reach for it again and I break your arm."

Something in the air cautions Tre not to do anything stupid. She knows he loves the power he is displaying right now. Perhaps a bit too much. In any case, he could do something to her. Finkle speaks up.

"Why don't you get the fuck outta here, Jamieson."

"You can't talk to me like that."

"What are you going to do about it? Spank me? "

Marshall Spence shoots Finkle a hateful glare. He snorts as he moves closer to Finkle, wrinkling his mustache, hoping he gets challenged. Finkle takes a few steps back. He fans his face with his hand, detecting the lingering aroma of apple cider spiked with vodka. Finkle can drink, but Marshall Spence's stench might add to his hangover. Marshall Spence suckles on his yellowing teeth as he returns his attention to Tre, who has moved between him and Finkle.

"You are under house arrest, Sheriff."

Finkle drops his hand in shock, and Tre is baffled.

"House arrest!" Finkle says.

"For what? Tre asks.

"After The Run last night, Mrs. Forgeron was found dead in her home. "

"Dead?" Finkle asks.

"How? I just saw her yesterday." Tre speaks up.

Marshall Spence moves Tre's weapon behind his back and places it in his belt between his shirt and trousers. She moves towards him again. He stops her and stares her down.

"When I discovered her, each eye was stitched into her palms and nailed to the trees so she could watch us. Her skin was removed from the top of her head to the tips of her toes and rolled into a nice little bundle beside her. I could bounce a penny from it because it was so elastic. Ants had begun stealing pieces of it, and I swear," He says. "It looked, and I bet it tasted, like Swiss cheese."

Tre stands like a statue trapped in a garden as a strong storm heads toward her. His words bounce off the walls of her brain, and like snapshots, images of Sadie—the Woman in the Woods— Mrs. Forgenon's body flash in her mind. Marshall Spence whispers near her ear: "I would hate to call your good old DA and worthless Captain."

Finkle steps in and stares Marshall Spence down. Marshall Spence laughs.

"I should have known that family is family. You shunned her and now look at you. Slobbering with the pig in the mud. You're dirty, Finkle. You've been dirty and always will be. Are you ready for what is about to come your way for doing this, because believe the Islanders will not be happy."

Making a face of disgust, Finkle leans back and says, "You smell of musty flesh and stupidity. Then again, you've always been that way, especially when I see you jerking off on the lake. You're a sick fuck."

"Not like you have sinned. Right, Finkle? It's amazing what happens when you're on the water."

"Put your dicks away. Why are you here, Marshall Spence, instead of finding the murderer?" Tre asks.

"Because we already have them. We just need a little more evidence, and they are going down."

"You can't honestly tell me you think it's Finkle. "

Surprised, Marshall Spence gives Tre a blank stare.

"It's you."

"Me? No. I never—I was there to talk about…"

"Katie told us."

The air in the foyer tightens as Tre and Finkle's heartbeats pound. Marshall Spence enjoys the fear and confusion in their eyes. Finkle stumbles back, white as a ghost and getting paler by the second and is grateful for the doorway he ends up leaning on so he doesn't fall. He doesn't want to give Marshall Spence the satisfaction of seeing him squirm. But he is.

"Katie?"

"Yeah, it's amazing. She's back. And she said she saw you murder her mother. On the night she came back. How can you be so cruel?"

Tre and Finkle exchange a look of confusion and concern. This is the point at which they realize Marshall Spence knows Finkle was the last person to see Katie alive. Many thoughts race through their heads, especially if Katie had ever left the island. What could she have been doing? Or who has been keeping her hidden?

"It's impossible. Katie, she…"

"Well, believe it Finkle. I'll be talking to you later. She never mentioned you, but when the shock wears off, I think she might have a grand ole story to share. So, until then," Marshall Spence turns his attention to Tre, "In fact, you are island-bound. I would like to keep my fellow Islanders safe from your craziness. Oh, I almost forgot." Marshall Spence hands Tre a folded piece of paper. "Since you're about procedures, I think you might get a kick out of this. It's a warrant."

Tre takes it. Marshall Spence chuckles, "Have a good day."

Deputies rush out of the house, their arms bulging with Tre's belongings. They take everything, from Levi's files to her Sheriff's uniforms. She observes as one deputy approaches and hands Marshall Spence a small box—the box Tre discovered in the Forgeron.

Tre approaches Finkle as he leans inside the doorway, still

stunned by what is happening. She rests her hand on his shoulder for comfort, but her gaze never leaves Marshall Spence. When he raises his eyebrows, the glisten within his eyes tells her everything. He knows.

"Well, I get to add breaking, and entering. Sheriff Finkle, I am surprised and in utter disgust you would take the law into your own hand like that. I believe you have something of Katie's, and she wants it back."

"Aren't you gonna do something?"

"Why would I do that when you're the one who brought the phone onto my island. I told you no cell phones were allowed on the island. I guess that just shows me that you still don't get it after all these years."

The junior deputies walk out, and Marshall Spence follows them toward the door. He stops and looks back at Tre and Finkle.

"Oh, and there's no need to join us for the feasting tonight, Tre being you're under house arrest of course. I'll let you know what happens." He is about to walk out when he turns back. "Oh, and to let you know. Someone saw Deputy Ollie in the woods alone last night. And no one has seen him since. Funny, isn't it."

Tre and Finkle exchange glances, talking without words. They know three things. One, Mrs. Forgeron is dead, and it was not by either of their hands, which means Tre is being set up. It can't be Marshall Spence. He's an asshole, not bright. Two, Katie Forgeron has returned after being missing for three years. As Islanders see it, another miracle. A miracle who is accusing Tre. And three, Ollie has mysteriously vanished.

As he turns to walk out the door, Marshall Spence turns his head halfway over his shoulder, and says, "If I find out you make even a milliliter of an attempt to leave, I will shoot to kill. Got it, Sheriff Finkle?"

"Go fuck yourself," Finkle says for Tre, which makes

Marshall Spence chuckle. "I think the sheriff can speak for herself."

"I did."

"Have a good night." Marshall Spence says as he walks down the porch steps, leaving Tre and Finkle alone.

"Are you thinking what I'm thinking?" Finkle asks.

Tre looks at Finkle.

"Probably not. But let's go with what you are thinking."

Tre walks into the foyer and looks out the window to see a few junior deputies watching her . Tre remains silent as she sets the pieces of what happened aside and prepares a roll of the dice plan.

"I need you to do something for me." Tre says.

───

Finkle walks down the dock while whistling a jolly tune. Fishermen on other boats watch with scowls as others shake their heads. Finkle waves at them as he walks onto his boat's deck. Finkle launches his boat like it's another day. The wind blows harshly and fast as he grows further away from Pine Island. He looks back. He lowers the speed and drops the anchor. He looks around as he releases three daily water cages with a splash. He glances around. He's alone. The other fishermen want nothing to do with him. Perfect.

───

"We need help. I have been keeping in touch with my office daily. When I don't reach out, they will be on their way. But I need you here. Be my eyes and ears and find Ollie."

───

He casts a glance at the murky, bobbing water. It looks cold and icy. "I hope I can out swim alligators."

He takes off his jacket, plaid shirt, and his boots. He dives in.

"What are you going to do?"

"Anything I can to look like I'm losing my mind as I find out what is happening around here. Plus, look at the files I have."

"I thought they took them."

"They did, but not the copies on my phone."

Tre lifts her mattress and grabs her backup phone. She searches her room for old boxes and discovers a small projector she remembers sending to her mother when she was alive. She opens the linen door and takes out a white sheet. She looks around upstairs and down looking for the darkest room. It turns out to be the study where she last spoke to her parents the night before she left. She begins to unfold the white sheet without hesitation. The projector's light is turned on, and after connecting to it, her phone begins to appear on the white sheet.

"All right, let's see what I'm missing."

CHAPTER 20
SHREDDING, RIBBONS, AND SALT

TABLES ARE attached end to end with savoy and sweet mouthwatering foods.

Large and flaky buttermilk biscuits sit next to sticks of freshly churned butter, pitchers of sweet tea have floating lemon rings, and a rack of ribs smolders, giving off the sweet aroma of the BBQ sauce coating it. The centerpiece waters mouth and eyes glisten of all who gaze upon it, an alligator arches upward with its jaw held open with sticks. It's leathery skin is decorated fruits and nuts before it's rips apart and ingested it like wild animals the Islanders. Whole cranberries sit in deep silver bowls with a long, curved fork to stab them. Brilliant red, black, blue, and green berries sparsely lay on the light brown, malted-colored handwoven strip that travels in the middle of all the tables.

Every islander stands behind the long-backed table chairs and listens to the children's choir sing. As the Islanders look on with delight, the choir's dark lyrics linger in the air. A small child with her hair in pigtails sings in high and low pitches, the salt and pepper shakers vibrate, causing the male Islanders to knock on the table every two beats, throwing the timing of the song off. The female Islanders take a step back, rest their hands on the curves of the chairs, then pull the chairs out to the side, letting the end of the legs gather dark soil beneath them. They bow, never looking up as the night slows and quiets.

The darkness moves forward and glides across the ground, covering it in a blanket of black thicker than the mist that hovers above it. The darkness advances along the ground covered in white baby's breath and pine straw. Eventually, darkness separates into individual blankets that are thicker and denser than fog. They are magnificent, statuesque, dark streams unfolding. Shadows break and rejoin with each sway, elongating the space.

Donned with animal skins and fur, the children's choir gradually morph from innocent to sinister. Their hands and feet pass through and replace the animals' paws which conceal their bloodstained flesh. Head to toe, their bodies are folded and sewn up in the bodies of foxes, cubs, dogs, skunks, and many more. The children continue to sing, moving the animal's mouths, and their eyes twinkle in the Christmas lights perching above them.

The smiles on the Islander's faces grow wider as their eyes narrow, and the white parts turn gray and dark as the children slow their songs, muttering disembodied words under their breath. The Islanders begin to sway as darkness approaches and takes their seats.

All the Islander men take their seats after the empty ones slide and pull themselves to the table's edge. The female Islanders rise from their bows, sit down, and pick up silver butter knives. They begin to dig out one of their eyes. Blood drops, but they never utter a sound as they cut and pull an eyeball out of its socket. They look at the dead one with their good eye before placing it inside their mouths. As they chew, pus oozes from their mouths, causing a squishy and rubbery crunch.

Finkle walks past the remnants of The Run, stepping over chains and rotting food with lanterns in both hands. To the left and right, the darkness is not as dense as it once was. The moon is close as it illuminates the shadowy areas. Pushing back his nerves and on the defensive, he trudges on.

Staring at the makeshift screen, Tre looks at each of the files, which she brings into focus. She leans forward and looks at the faces of the missing. Then, she notices a few have come back.

Colby's family picture shows him with his mother and brother by the lakeside, holding up a fish they caught. Katie was on the porch, churning butter and smiling as she sat in the rocking chair her father made her. Isaiah stood with his arms over Finkle's shoulder while standing on the dock of Finkle's boat, with the wind blowing both of their hairs backward. The oldest picture is of the Dodson Twins, in the same position in the same place, old and new taken in front of the town general store. The last is The Woman in the Woods, dead and hanging on the log—taken by Ollie.

She steps back and takes a good, long look. Her eyes dart between all of them. That's when she sees it.

There is pepper in the woman's hand and salt in the man's hand, but neither says anything. The children knelt with their heads down, impersonating the animal they were supposed to be, the silent roar of a bear, the soaring of a hawk, the scrambling of a fox, the tall king-like stance of a lion.

The female Islanders dump small amounts of pepper into a small mound as the male Islanders pass the salt down the table. Before the next man takes the salt, they make a circle with their hands. The women begin to rumble and blow through their lips, releasing a small amount of pepper bit by bit.

Low and haunting, a monstrous hum grows louder as the salt is passed down the table faster and faster. The women throw the remaining pepper away. They then slam the glass pepper container on the table harder and harder. The children sway back and forth, creeping in a small circle with a low growl.

With his lantern as his weapon, Finkle listens to the male laughter circle him. He can't see the male but he twirls in place trying to keep up but more importantly stay on guard. To the left of him, twigs break. To his right, heavy and fast footsteps behind him make him turn around, and yet no one is there. But he catches something from the corner of his eye. A long white figure slips back behind a thick tree. He doesn't waste time and heads straight for it. It could be Ollie, lost and confused.

"Ollie? Ollie, is that you? I know this place is getting to you, but we have to help Tre out and get the both of you back to the mainland."

Finkle slides himself around the tree and approaches a well-lit section of the woods. He raises the lantern to illuminate his face and eyes, which are wider than his drinking stomach could ever be.

"Oh my god."

An altar sat amid blackened tree logs in a circle as animal's eyeballs, and tongues lay in wooden bowls along the trail of scorch marks, some emanating light streams of smoke. The food he has been eating can be seen in his hollowed-out stomach Bread, potato soup, and apple pie—all covered in maggots. His eyes are twisted like a screw, his lips split from two to four, and his teeth have been plucked and replaced with his fingernails. His teeth hang from around his neck like a necklace.

———

Small Christmas presents can be seen in the background in the picture Tre is looks at. She recalls a tradition in which the ancestors would bring a gift to one of the lucky ones. A knock comes at the door. Tre takes a step back and looks at her door. Another thud. She enters the foyer and places her hand on the doorknob. Another thud. She draws in a deep breath.

———

Levi opens the door. He sees no one as the cricket chirp. He uses the doorframe to hold on to as he leans out, looking left and right. No one is there.

"Hello?"

He starts back inside, still seeing no one, and that's when he looks down. A small box with a Christmas tag that reads, *To Levi,* is staring back at him in his house's doorway. Surprised and honored, he looks up to the nights sky, smiling as if an angel kissed him, he closes his eyes.

"I knew you were listening."

The lid shuffles. In anticipation, Levi bites the grooves of his bottom lip, as he manages to get it off. He looks inside and gasps. He reaches inside and retrieves the gift, dropping the box in excitement.

It's a simple blue ribbon.

"Levi! Levi, put it back."

Tre accelerates as she speeds down Levi's driveway. Levi doesn't hear her as the faint hum of the wedding procession draws him into another dimension. He rubs the silky ribbon between his thumb and palm as a dreamy grin spread his face, causing the music to grow louder the longer he holds it. The ribbon is a wedding ring for an islander. The moment it is wrapped around a woman's right ring finger, her heartbeats instantly connect her to the man she is now married to, regardless of whether they exchanged vows. His ancestors have given him a second chance he never had, but always wanted. Tre is to be married. All she has to do is allow him to tie it.

"Levi!"

"You're here."

They are meant to be, as her father told him when he was a teenager. Tre has finally arrived to cement their bond. As she rushes up to him, he turns to face her and waits. She slams into him so hard that he nearly drops the ribbon. She wraps her arms around his neck, and he happily does the same. He squeezes his arms tightly around her body as he listens to her try to catch her breath.

"I can't believe you came."

"Listen to me, Levi. Every single person who has gone missing and come back or has had something restored got a present from the ancestors during The Shredding."

"I love you so much, Tre. I want to spend the rest of my life with you."

Levi gets down on one knee and presents her with the ribbon. She looks at him, puzzled, and knows he's not listening to her.

"Are you insane? Every person who has…"

"It doesn't matter. It's my time. And I am not going to waste it talking about such little things. Our ancestors want us to be together. And I agree with them."

Tre grabs him and pulls him up. But the delusional look won't leave his face no matter what she says. As far as Levi is concerned, Tre is confessing her love and loyalty, saying she will never leave again.

"The second you opened that present you let something

loose and now it's coming for you. It's like completing some sort of ritual."

"I love you, Tre. Marry me and I will make you the happiest descendant on this island. Will you marry me?"

Tre knows he's lost in the island's traditions because of his glazed-over eyes and ominous expression. The customs of The Shredding.

"No, I'm not going to marry you."

Levi's heart begins to ache and his face falls. He lowers his gaze to the ribbon. The pretty baby blue fades as it blackens and absorbs into his skin. Tre takes a step back.

"I'm sorry, Levi. I really am."

Levi takes a step forward and grabs his chest. In pain, he stumbles and falters on his feet. Tre attempts to assist, but it is too late. A small pop sounds out.

Levi's heart explodes.

He collapses to his knees and dies face-first on the porch.

Terrified and backing up, Tre misses a step and lands on the ground. She pushes herself back, but she can't get away from Levi's dead gaze. The fear is real. It calls out to her.

The house is still and quiet. A small brown rabbit with a bushy white tail hops happily in the garden, gnawing on the green grass and on the pink, yellow, and white flower petals. It flicks its ears as a light wind brushes against them, and its whiskers shake as it finishes its mid-morning meal. A high-pitched shrill bounce off the sides of the air like ping pong in an endless game between two adversaries. The frightened rabbit scurries away across the field.

Another scream, this time a little lower and more from the gut, as wind rushes toward the porch. Blinds shake, and curtains try to escape the desperate but unnatural sound emanating from Tre and Finkle's parents' house. Hollow thuds begin to sound in a succession of three, each time getting harder and denser every few minutes on the track as a black record turn with the player's needle sliding in and out in its middle while slowly scratching it.

In the foyer, shattered glass from a baking dish lies among nutty and chocolate brownies that have been squished and stepped on. The framed pictures, which were on the wall, are knocked off and scattered everywhere on the stairs and over the railing. They reveal the dusty and unclean walls behind where the frames sat. Moving up the stairs, the brownies make their way up the steps, disappearing the further it goes up. But there's something different. They are not normal. The footprints aren't normal. They are hooved. Embedded in the banister, a deep scratch starts at the bottom rail and makes their way up, leaving the wood carved in five continuous spirals. None of them are broken, and the spirals are clean and tight, ending at the top.

Under the closed bedroom door's cracks, the sun beats through, casting a shadow of the door's frame on the dark hallway. The thud continues, ending with a guttural, painful roar. Three thuds. One caw. The needle scratches loudly on the record. The caw grows deep. The needle digs deeper. Torn and missing their soles, a pair of shoes sit to the right inside the first bedroom. Solid, hard, the three thumps turn to two. In a curved pattern, shreds of blue and white fabric are small clumps that decorate the upstairs hallway, which turn to drops of blood. There are parts where the blood has seeped into the light-colored wooden floor, discoloring, and darkening it.

———

A single lamp sits on a table end, its white shade splattered red as the wall, and wobbles on its legs as the thuds causing it to act like a music counter.

At the end of the hallway, the two lights at the top of the wall flicker as Sabine slams her head against the wall. Every time she leans forward, her forehead is covered in bright red blood. But on the sides of her face and her clothes, her blood is dark red and dried. Her nose is barely visible, her hair is clumpy and gathered at the ends, her lips are split, and at her feet, a few teeth lay on the floor and in the blood. With blood gathered in her throat, she gurgles, and some dribbles from her mouth and down her chin as she lets out another deep shrill like a banshee. She arcs her neck as far as it can go, almost touching between her shoulder blades. Blood streams across her white eyes as the veins in her neck bulge. Suddenly, Sabine snaps her neck and slams her head into the wall one last time as the record player stops mid-scratch. Slowly, she places her splinter-filled fingers on the wall and takes a few deep breaths. She begins laughing, low and hyena-like.

"Sabine!"

Tre's voice rings out around Sabine, and she claws at her face and grabs clumps of her hair out. She moves her gaze to the side. Cracking her neck, she drops her arms, allowing them to fall heavy and hard beside her, leaving bloody prints on the wall. As she makes her way to the stairs, she steps over the limbs of animals.

"Coming ma'am."

CHAPTER 21
BEGINNING OF THE END

THOSE TWO FINKLES DON'T GIVE A FUCK

FINKLE AND TRE chase each other through the woods, both running from something behind them. Neither of them looks back as they enter the fields, where their family home stands in the center. Finkle abruptly came to a halt. He kneels down, gasping for air, and rests his hand on his knees. Tre returns his gaze. She comes to a halt.

"Come on. We gotta get out of here."

"Why? It's going to catch up with us. It has before."

"And you're going to let it. I don't give a fuck what's in the dark. All I know is that this time I'm going to leave you. So, man the fuck up, and let's go."

She begins to walk off. Finkle stands. He steps to move. He can't. He looks down and freezes.

"Tre?"

"I have that extra phone I collected from Katie in my room…"

In Tre's bedroom a circle-shaped light bobs in the window. As its sheen darkens, Tre sees herself staring at her. The other Tre shows her Katie's phone, smiling. The other Tre opens her mouth and drops the phone inside. With a hard swallow, the phone is gone. She licks her fingers like she just ate a delicious and succulent meal.

"Tre. Tre!"

"What is it?"

Tre spins around to see Finkle still looking down. Finkle and Tre's hearts beat in unison for a moment. They are silent as the darkness encircles his ankles. Laces with long, shiny, and sharp black claws intertwine within his boot. The darkness creeps up his lower leg like a spider climbing a wall. As he raises his head to face her, the color on his face fades. She takes a step forward, but he throws his hand in the air and holding still. She can see his hand muscles twinge and flex at her as she tries to move again. Finkle stops her as the pieces of darkness grow tighter in their grip. Tre knows she should charge at him, but she's not sure darkness would let go and leave.

As sweat rolls down his face, Finkle says in a quiet voice, "Run."

Finkle is yanked backward by his ankles and immediately dragged back toward the woods.

"Jacob!" Tre screams as she takes off after him.

Finkle screams as he tries to stop himself. He digs his fingers into the ground. Three fingers on one hand snapped to the side and were instantly broken. But that doesn't stop him. He reaches out to the grass, only to pull it out, it never helps him. Tre runs as fast as she can to catch up. The closer he gets to the tree line. The further Tre falls back. With her side hurting and throbbing in pain, she refuses to stop. Then Finkle disappears into the darkness, as do his screams.

Tre grabs ahold of her side and stops. She searches for any sign of him. Silence. She takes a few steps backward and then heads for her house.

Tre trips as she runs up the stairs and bursts through the front door. The door hits the wall inside as she rushes up the stairs.

She stops at her door. Swinging back and forth for a couple of seconds, she pumps herself up for the lookalike she keeps seeing before she throws open the door ready to fight. No one is there. The small light she saw from the field was the light-bulb on her nightstand. Not believing what she witnessed, that Katie's phone was eaten, she starts to look for it.

The wood inside the small dresser drawer slides apart loudly as she yanks it out. It's empty. Katie's cell phone isn't there.

"Fuck!"

She drops the drawer and runs out. She busts through Ollie's bedroom door. Marshall Spence might have taken Ollie's suitcases and everything else he bought from the mainland. But he never took the one thing Tre always taught Ollie to hide since the day he became her deputy.

———

Tre stands with Ollie at the coffee pot in the Sheriff's station on the mainland. She stirs her creamer in with a red straw. She takes it out and chews on it as they begin to walk.

"It's simple. Never have just one."

"Never have just one," Ollie repeats as he jots it down. "Got it."

Tre stops him and says, "Make sure you have it somewhere no one would ever find it. Whether that's on your body or in a special spot in a room. Look at me. I have two on me right now."

Tre steps back and points them out.

"Ankle and waist, of course. But I have three hidden in my office."

"Why so many?"

"You can never be too careful."

Tre walks off as Ollie repeats as he writes that down.

"You can never be too careful. Got it."

———

Aggressively, Tre pushes back the remainder of Ollie's clothes, which are hanging off the closet rod. She places her hands on the high shelf. Nothing. She bends down and begins to pop the tops off of some boxes inside. Tissue paper, hats, old shoes with golden buckles, and thick wool scarves She stops. She listens to what is happening downstairs. What she doesn't know is that the darkness inside the closet reaches out to her, barely touching her hair. It wants to, but something stops it. Hearing nothing, she continues to pull and open more boxes from inside. She opens the lid of the last box. She pauses and looks.

"Glad you took notes, Ollie."

She reaches inside and retrieves a black and silver Glock 9MM. She checks the bullet intake. It's full. She grabs the extra magazine and puts it in her back pocket. She rushes down the stairs with the gun in her hands, ready for anything as she heads for the front door and into the night.

A woman's hums stop her as she is about to slam the door behind her. Her breath was kicked out of her. She knows that song. It's one from her childhood. Twinkle, Twinkle, Little Star. Her other half would sing it to her when she was sick, upset, or if she thought she needed to hear it. She listens to the breathy tones of the female voice and the deep melody.

"Momma?" she says to herself, softly.

Tre turns to the living room. She listens, and her mother's laughter comes from inside. Tre walks slowly and gets closer, where she sees the flicker of light from the fireplace against the back wall. She peeks her head around the corner to see her mother's dark bun slightly moving as her hums begin again.

"Momma?"

The movement of the dark black bun stops. It tilts up toward the left.

"Theresa? Is that you, dear? It's late. Why aren't you in bed like a good little girl?"

Her body weakens with every step she takes toward the melodies of her mother's voice and Ollie's Glock dangles in her hand. A single tear rolls down Tre's flushing cheek. Logical reasoning suggests her mother has been dead for many years. She's seen her grave. Even in death, she has heard stories of how she was disowned and shunned the second her heart stopped. But how can one be sure when she is here, talking to Tre?

"I'm sorry momma. I lost track of time."

"Oh, it's all right. Why don't you come and sit down with me by the fire before you catch a cold? The air shoots daggers this time of year, and the night turns darker earlier. I wouldn't want you to get lost."

Tre's shadow covers the back wall as she moves to the white cushioned chairs caddy-cornered to her mother. Placing Ollie's Glock on the small circular table between the chairs, Tre sits down, and listens to the knitting needles her mother is using. They hit and scratch against one another as she makes loop after loop. Tre slumps, her eyes wide. Her mother's light blue eyes sparkle but fade and turn black as she picks up her teacup. Following the red lipstick indentation, she takes a sip and lets out an "Ah."

"Nothing like jasmine and lavender to end the night. Don't you think, Theresa?"

"Is this some kind of joke?" Tre snaps with her brows narrowed and growls in her lip. She knows her other is the darkness.

"I assure you. None of this is a joke."

"This isn't funny, Sabine."

Sabine takes another sip of her tea. As she pulls it back, a mischievous smile fades as she sits looking at Tre, who grows angrier as every second passes. She hands Tre a cup.

"Here. You always drank tea with your mother before you went to bed."

"You're not my mother. Why did you sound like her? Or talk to me in her voice?"

Sabine chuckles, and says, "Dear child. I told your father you were the smart one out of the two. But I fear I could have been wrong. Here. Drink some tea."

"Do I look like I'm fucking Alice in Wonderland?" Tre says, fierce and intense.

Sabine's glee and sweetness fade as the teacup shakes in her hand. Tre turns away and rises from her seat.

"Sit down, Theresa."

Turning to leave, Tre stops as the other Tre from the woods is standing in front of her. Before she can react, her lookalike blows a handful of herbs. Specks of rosemary and thyme coat the top layer of her eyes, blinding her, and a few buds of cloves embed themselves down her throat and numb her voice box. Her lookalike's grim smile widens with excitement as she steps closer to Tre and pushes her backward. For Tre, she feels like she is falling down a well as the light dissipates into darkness. But she never hits the bottom, instead, she falls back into the cushioned chair.

"Now where was I? Oh, yes. Tea."

Tre sits confused and unsettled as she watches through the haze, her lookalike bending downward to Sabine making her chuckle.

"Oh, you. Now be gone and get ready," Sabine tells her.

Sabine turns to Tre who is paralyzed, not just in fear but by the cloves rushing through her body, pricking, and numbing her muscles.

"I want to tell you a story. The story your grandmother never finished. God rest her soul. Everything she said was true. We came to be…well, it was not your usual love story. Yes, I know a love story. Not between two strangers, but two siblings."

Tre's body starts giving off unusual jerks, causing her shoulder and leg joints to crack as her spine twists and turns slowly and deeply. Sabine closes her eyes, listening and loving every sound. Sabine watches as Tre tries to mumble. The fire's flame brightens, the scent of rotten eggs fills the air, and Sabine's tone turns sinister as her eyes narrow.

"Oh, no. Not like that. It was a love of family. The desire for respect and the need for what was owed."

CHAPTER 22
THE BEGINNING OF
THE LOST

A STREAM of urine hits the wobbly half-moon, reflecting off the water's edge. With a loud "Ah," the man dressed in 1800 clothing can't seem to stop. He wears a pair of brown boots just below the knee. A tweed vest perfectly buttoned down with gold-like buttons that match the cuff on his long white sleeve, with an overcoat with a long tail split at the end of his spine, that hangs over his noble tight ass.

Shaking his small pecker, which resembles a Vienna sausage, James "Short Round" Thomas, wonders what the hell he did with his beer. Suddenly, he is slapped on the back and nearly topples forward as a friend, Charles, a heavy-set man dressed in all black, laughs at the bad joke another friend, Bean Pole, told him. Behind them, the final man, Frankie, sits on the sand laughing as he feels the cool wind coming off the water. Charles hands Short Round an amber-red bottle filled with whiskey. Of course, they swiped it as they left the bar after being thrown out for being too rough with the prostitutes.

"Then I was be gone, old man. Can't you see what I am doing?" Charles mocks as he humps the air, making sure his big belly bounces.

Shaking the last of his urine from his hand, Short Round

zips his pants and steals the bottle, finishing the whiskey for himself. But there is nothing inside. He taps the bottom, hoping for that last drop, but it never comes.

"What shall we do now? Sleep it off on the sand before making our way to our wives?" Bean Pole says.

"Our nagging wives with tongues like silk in public, but daggers in the bed."

"Oh, I've your wife in the alley with another, Slouching her spit on another knob before coming home to you at night," Charles squawks at Bean Pole.

Anger wells up in Bean Pole's face as his cheeks redden, and he grips the sand to help him up as the alcohol flows through his veins, infecting his mobility. He lunges at the heavyset man. He misses and lands in the water. Face first. The three remaining men whoop and holler at the stupidity of the drunk man, even making jokes about how he will wash out into the water like a piece of driftwood.

Throwing the empty bottles to the left and right of them, the men help Bean Pole up and dust off the water dripping from his face. Confusion and stupidity are high in this group, along with a dangerous pattern of women and drinks. Then Frankie catches a flame coming from the other side of the water, from the island.

As young men, they were told not to cross the water. It did not matter if they heard the flickering flames sing chants or songs. When they were asked if anyone had ever waded the water before, they were told those who had never returned.

"I don't want to go home to my nagging wife." I want to go there," Frankie says, pointing to the flickering flame.

The three other men looked at him. With fear in their eyes, they easily shy away, shaking their heads and waving the idea away. Frankie stands in the lake's waves, which are hitting his knees.

"Well, I'm going," Frankie shouts from the distance as he trudges through the water towards the docks. There he unties a small rowboat and begins to push off the wooden poles. Charles grabs the side as Bean Pole and Short Round climb in.

"If you're going, we all go."

As the flame from the bonfire flickers, women, naked, gracefully dance around the fire, humming songs in tune with the waves of the lake. Through the moonlight, their wrinkles seem smoother the longer they twirl in a circle together. Two women clasp hands as they laugh, feeling the wind cover their breasts and travel down the bubbles of their spines. Glistening in the sweat of the fire, an old woman with saggy breasts, three double chins, and thick thighs stands and sways back and forth. As she does, her body changes. The wrinkles drop and roll down her body; three double chins zero out as her skin tightens and blushes like a blooming rose. Her wiry silver hair becomes saturated in the pine color, brown with highlights of copper hues. She stops and then sends a kiss toward the bushes where Charles is hiding. He can't help but emerge from the bushes, excited and hard.

The women scream and disperse down the pathways hidden from the men. Charles stomps his feet like a dog running in place and shifts his head back and forth, trying to decide whom to chase. He picked the left one, the one who blew the kiss, and dashed down a path.

To the right, Bean Pole dodges the tree limbs after one of the women giggles and covers her breast with her slender and sharp fingernails. He loves the chase, but she loves it more. She teases him by giving him a nipple slip. It revs him up.

Short Round runs like a merry go round along the women's footsteps around the fire. With each turn, the woman and he grow further and further away until they blend into the tree line.

Frankie calmly steps out of the bushes and examines his

surroundings. He listens to the water crashing, the wind skimming the water's surface, and the pine straw dropping around him. A figure on the other side of the fire draws his attention as he turns his head from right to left.

Through the flames, he notices a female wearing a white, lacy gown hovering just above her ankles and bare feet It's Emme, and she is stunning. Her long black hair is the color of raven wings, and her skin is light and delicate. She twirls around as Frankie approaches the fire for a better look.

"Do you like what you see?' Emme asks.

All Frankie could do was smile, drool dripping down his chin like a dog in heat. As the shoulder part of her dress slips, he steps in front of her, and she grabs it before anything else can be seen. He smiles innocently at her, and the batting of her lashes turns him on.

"Are you from these parts?" Emme looks him up and down. She settles her hand over the tip of his pants, and slowly massages it.

"I am," he replies as he grabs her neck, and snaps it in place as he aggressively kisses it.

"Why haven't I seen you here before?" she says breathlessly.

"I'm from the mainland," he whispers in her ear as he pins her lobe between his teeth.

As quickly as she started, she stopped. Frankie is disappointed when she drops the ends of her dress and furrows her brow. The softness and sweetness of her voice fades.

"You're not allowed here."

"I know. But your charm called, and here I am."

"You must leave before it's too late."

"Too late for what?"

"Before your wife finds out."

Emme takes off running, slamming into the trees as she goes. As Frankie pursues her, the branches lower and block him. When Emme looks back, she sees him fight and break the limbs. She is horrified by this scene. Something inside her tugs on her arm, and she accelerates her escape run. Frankie has no idea what is going on, but he is also speeding up. A small amount of rage bubbles from the bottom of his gut with each step.

"Why are you running away? Stop! Stop, I say."

She has a good lead on him, so she turns in her run. She settles her feet into the bundle of leaves. Frankie appears through the dark hole in the trees, and smiles at her.

"Why are you running from me?"

"Anula. Sperati. Gulnara."

Finishing her chant, she kicks the leaves off her foot. In the middle of the air, each leaf slowly separates and shatters into ash. Frankie watches as she raises her hand and blows it on her palm. From her lips, a breeze sends the ashes toward him. He is hit in the chest with the force of a thousand pebbles. He flies backward. He lands on his back, knocking the breath from him, and then begins to wipe off the ashes before they continue burning through his coat and shirt, piercing his skin. Smirking, she enjoys listening to his fright and agony. She turns her back to leave.

Suddenly, the birds above her scattered at the sound of a gunshot. She turns her head back toward Frankie. He is leaning forward on the middle of his back, heavily breathing, and a stream of smoke travels between his eyes. She follows the stream to a gun, the barrel smoking, and pointed at her. She looks down at her chest. Seeing nothing, she places her right hand's fingers between her breasts and pulls back.

Coated in red, she looks bewildered as she dips her head down. From the middle of her chest, a stream of red sketches itself down the white gown. Like a top spinning, she becomes dizzy and eventually drops to her knees. In rapid suctions, her breaths quicken and slow, quicken and slow. She drops onto her stomach. The ground shakes. She doesn't have the strength to gather dirt under her nails.

Frankie stands up. He approaches her as she gasps for air and tries to crawl. Even with a hole in her chest, she recognizes the danger she is in. Frankie steps over her in a backward straddle and admires her while scratching the back of his head with the gun. He nods his head in agreement with his inner voice, huffing. He starts reloading his gun.

As she fears for her life, she inhales more dirt. She can see the trees reach out to her, wanting to help. She calms down. She hears the click of Frankie's gun as he prepares to fire. She shuts her eyes. A single tear falls and darkens the dirt beneath. He fires a shot.

She blinks and opens her eyes. She listens behind her as Frankie gurgles and a tear falls off her cheek and hovers in the night air. He falls silent. She is flipped over and placed in the arms of a man without warning. But not just any ordinary man. It's Stanley, drenched in blood, the majority of which smeared around his mouth. They are a year apart and are said to be closer together than the earth and the moon. Every step made, another follows, not closely behind, but beside.

"Soeur? Soeur? Vous m'entendez?" (Sister? Sister? Can you hear me?")

"Je t'aime," (I love you,) breaks from Emme's lips, still gasping for air.

Emme tries to raise her hand. Instinctively, Stanely slips it into his hand and brings it up to his cheek, where he rests it against it. Her eyes slowly begin to glaze over. He held her hand tighter. Emme goes limp. Trembling, her body shakes inside his arms as he tries to wake her. Tears streamed down Stanley's bloodstained cheeks. When he turns his head up to the night sky, he roars. The roar is deep and loud, shaking the trees and causing the stars to crash into the water and the moon to hide.

Bean Pole is bent out of shape with his arms twisted, legs twirling around his waist, and tongue hanging out the side of his mouth. An animal like a woman is draped over his body and feeding on his lower intestines. Hearing the roar, she turns her head and takes off, dragging the intestines until they rip out of his stomach.

Stanley holds Emme close, his cries quieting down as he whispers in her ear. To this day, no one knows exactly what he said. The rumors always mention something beastly and against all laws of nature, as the religious world would say. While others believe it was nothing except the words of an apology for not being around at the right time. Stanley lays her down gently as his howls dissipate.

The grass below his toes never makes a sound, even though it is drying and breaking. The wind sways the leaves, and some even fall, but the silence is deafening. Emerging from the dark soil, scorpions and beetles larger than his hand fall into an imaginary line as the darkness folds Emme inside it. The blood stain of the man he killed slowly sinks into his skin, flushing it with a splatter of blush only he knows as his eyes darken and deepen inside their sockets.

He makes a fist, then loosens his fingers, and makes a crosswise and downward symbol in the dirt. Soon, he appears to float in the dark, with shadows covering half of his body, revealing a monster with sharp fangs, and whittling brows. A deep, savage, hateful growl erupts from his gut. He allows the wolf within him to emerge, hungry and hateful.

CHAPTER 23
A STOPPED CLOCK IS RIGHT TWICE A DAY

ON THE MAINLAND, men armed with silver, guns, and pitchforks hurry to the lake. Nervous, they look at each other. They never thought anyone would break the treaty. A treaty that was written into existence hundreds of years before the town was built. They were warned. Share the waters, but never travel over them. With axes and other kinds of tools they call weapons resting on their shoulders, the gaggle of men make their way home, walking slowly and dragging their worn-out bodies behind them. In the front, the priest watches the men falling back in a slow stride, into the warming arms of their wives, listens to the cheers of their children, and sees their elders' smiling faces as they head toward their homes. The priest approaches the church at the end of the road.

A brief and powerful scream fills the air as a man steps out of his house carries his dead wife's slashed body. The priest rushes over only to slide in the dirt, stopping as another man screams with a bloody blanket covering half his body. Another man walks out with his wife's bloody apron hanging from his shaking hands. Soon, the road becomes flooded with blood, wails, and bodies. In the distance, three large stakes sit in the middle of the small open field, where the children play chase and town picnics happen after every sermon, sung by the choir made of the sweet and off-key voices of the children, the future.

The bodies belonged to the Priest's church family, or what he called his Inquirers. On the stake to his right, a twenty-year-old man whose family died of a fever caught by small worms contracted through the water when he was a child. The Priest took him in because he had a need to show kindness and love to those less fortunate. On the left stake, his old friend since they were babies stares at him with hollowed-out eyes and a rope embedded into his chest, holding up his saggy breasts. He loved him so much and never wanted the friendship to end. But the middle stake broke the Priest's heart, the spinster of the town.

She was crippled in the left hand from birth, a defect no one knew, let alone understood, so she was condemned and said to be unworthy of marriage, children, and love. But for the priest, she was a kindred spirit. A relationship they hid from the town and his followers. Her stomach hangs open, and her head hangs, staring at him with the tip of a cross sticking out the top of her head. A warning, no. No, not a threat. A spell, but not a spell of not being able to walk, talk or speak. But a blood spell for a lost love, then everyone else must lose a love as well, the closest to them all. For the priest, he had three loves.

The priest notices the men bringing out their family members, wailing in pain and anguish, as if in slow motion. The bodies pile up over the course of hours, which seems like minutes to the priest. It's as if a plague struck the town, and they had to burn the bodies to rid themselves of the disease.

The priest's hidden love is at the top of the list. Is this some sort of karma? He was finally caught up in a sin. His sin. Late nights of praying together resulted in him pressing her body against the pulpit, letting tears fall down his cheeks as he orgasms hard and deep inside her as she bends back as far as she can go, touching the floor and singing a hymn. He's failed. He is an embarrassment. A man in sin, he slams his fist in agreement with the word every night. Liar. Turning away, he walks through the town's men who are waiting to hear what to do, anger boiling within him. He is no longer a man of God. He wants revenge.

The priest commands attention and lets his voice echo through the approaching night. There are no stars or moon, the ideal disguise.

———

Standing on the edge of the water's edge, in line with Stanley —half man, half wolf—the doppelgangers, or what mainlanders call the Dark Descendants, wait. The war they have been waiting for is about to happen as the priest and townsmen hold their ground. Stanley tilts his head. Nothing needs to be said as his smile fades into the shadows. The priest steps forward. He takes the necklace, holds out a cross with golden thorns, and points it at Stanley. He scoffs, and a guttural growl begins.

"You shall pay for the innocence you have stolen," The Priest yells with authority.

"We will wander around in the darkness until we are found. One by one we will wait for the lives of our kin, who will continue the death of yours."

"The devil be glad for your arrival." A man standing behind the Priest snaps.

Hissing and cracking, a woman licking her fingers replies, "Your wife will be fresh again as I chew her tongue and suckle her breast as a baby she birthed."

The man begins to step but is stopped by the Priest as he quietly says, "Be humble in her name, but rage in your heart."

Slowly, the priest turns, his rage visible in his narrowed eyes as Stanley raises his arms and tilts his head toward the dark sky. The Dark Descendants do the same thing. The priest and the men yell and lunge at them.

"Don't be afraid of the dark, but what's in the dark," Stanley whispers.

Sabine stares into the fire's flames as they slow and die. She makes a face because the taste is bitter.

"The slaughter was one that the men thought was their idea. When in turn, it was the dark descendants."

"Witches?"

Delighted, Sabine turns to Tre, and says, "I hear your voice is back. I told you her spells never last long. She isn't as powerful as she once was."

"Who's she?"

Sabine's sigh extinguishes the last of the flames as she slumps back against the chair. Disappointed, she slams her hand hard against the arms of the chair. She shook her head and leaned her chin against her chest.

"Have you been listening? Because we have been talking about her. The sister. The Founding Fathers in a sense. The influence who has millions of people watching their every move."

The feeling in Tre's fingers is slowly coming back. The sting is unbearable. But she doesn't dare let Sabine know.

"I know she's a witch. But what was her name?"

"Oh," Sabine laughs. "You're not as dumb as your father thought. Thank goodness for that. I'm glad some of your mother rubbed off. Speaking of your mother. She was a witch. Well, not a very good one. The spell she practiced every single day failed every single day."

"What did you do to her?"

"It's not what I did, it's how I helped. If you're going to take care of your husband's needs, then someone does. She just happened to catch us. As that saying goes, she had to go. Burying her in the unholy ground was just the first step in getting you back."

Sabine stands and leans down toward Tre.

"I mean, she never came to have dinner with you and Finkle, did she? I don't think so. I couldn't have her warning you."

"You killed her?"

Sabine slaps Tre in the middle of her forehead, so hard her neck snaps. But it doesn't break. Pain radiates on all areas of her neck as Sabine stands and leans against the mantle.

"That hurt, you fucking bitch."

"Kisses and hugs. That's how you ended every letter. You know she wrote back to you. Once. I was the one who was supposed to deliver it. I didn't. Let me tell you what it said."

From her apron pocket, Sabine slips a folded letter out. She flips it around, but nothing is on it. She flips it again and two words appear.

"Test time."

"What the fuck does that…"

Before Tre can finish, a long black arm appears between her legs and slams its long black claws inside her leg, a rip sounding through the room. She yells. Another arm rips from the left side of the chair, its claws embedded in her forearm. A third arm reaches from the back of the chair and around her shoulder, slowly digging its claws into the back of her shoulder, blood seeping out. Tre fights to break free, yanking at her arms as the claws on her leg dig deeper, making her wince. Sabine crumples the paper and tosses it into the fire with her arm across her chest. Tre is turned away from the light of the fire by the chair. It rushes forward, facing the bay window, and Tre screams as the chair shatters the glass, shards crashing into her lap and nicking her. The flame left in Sabine's eyes dims as the fire burns out.

"Darkness has no sound until someone gives it to them."

Full speed ahead, the chair travels through the woods. The pine straw attaches itself to the bottom of the chair like sap, and branches reach out for a touch—not of the chair, but of Tre. As she continues to struggle, there's no way she's breaking free. She attempts to scream, but her voice is stolen by the wind. Sharp turns jerk the chair, ending up on the black pavement of the main road. The chair passes a few islanders as they stand with torches like they are in the military. As Tre passes, they step forward and begin walking together in three lines.

An aerial view of Pine Island from a plane high in the sky would reveal the strange design. The torches of the islanders would follow the edge of the sickle. Slowly, making their way to the tip. They would never see Tre and the chair, as the darkness would make sure they couldn't. But the torches would be like a child's flashlight game.

Marshall Spence steps into the road. He eagerly waits for Tre to appear. Before he knows it, Tre's chair stops in front of him with a jerk. She looks up.

"Jamieson?"

"It's Marshall Spence."

Marshall Spence knocks Tre out with a punch to the face. As he straddles her lap, he shakes his hand. He pulls her head up by her hair and yanks her eyes open. She is not awake. He smiles as he accepts a torch and steps aside. The chair moves slowly along its path as Marshall Spence falls in line with the rest of the islanders.

After what seems like hours, Tre moans in pain. Single-laced ropes are tied around each of her wrists, and thick black belts wrap around her waist, chest, and legs, with the legs fastened down and laced with herbs. The smell is sweet, earthy, and pleasant. It's a dunking booth. She hovers over the lake water. Surrounded by silence, she turns to see the islanders staring at her, holding torches and as still as statues. The silence is disturbing.

Out of nowhere, Finkle appears. Tripping into the water, he hits the wood of the chair. He begins to loosen the knots around Tre's wrists. But they are so tight, they won't budge.

"Finkle. I think something is wrong with them. Like a trance or something."

"I don't know and don't care."

He pulls on the loose end of a rope, only to lose his grip, and gives himself a rope burn. He moves to the belt and undoes the one on her legs. He moves up to the one on her waist.

"Your knife."

Tre sees his hair is shiny, and his jean jacket is darker as if it's damp, and his boots are gone. He's never been barefoot a day in his life. "I can't find it. I must have lost it."

He leans into her as he attempts to untie her hands, but she knows something is different about him. His hair seems longer in the back than it was a few hours ago. His smell isn't of the shrimp, crawfish, or lobsters he gathers, it's more like oak and leather. Tre looks around to see the Islander's keep still. She hears the flicker of the torches only. And the breathing coming from herself.

"Why aren't they stopping you?"

Finkle stops. He leans back. He looks down at Tre. He pokes at her cheek and slides off her. His feet step into the water and he walks to the small opening between him, the islanders, and Tre.

"I had you going, didn't I?"

Speechless, Tre stares as her eyes widen in confusion as members of the coven begin to clap for Finkle. A deputy cheers for Finkle while the other deputies whistle at him. A few women holler and cheer for him as well. He walks around in the area, shy and occasionally waving at them with a slightly embarrassing smile.

"I'm a fantastic actor. Or so I'm told," he tells Tre.

Every sixth islander walks in the middle right behind Fickle, and he walks in a semi-small circle, bowing and thanking them for their support. They place the torches down and form a spiral, instead of inside out, it's outward in, a symbol representing the coven and the darkness.

"I wish you could see your face. I know."

Marshall Spence tosses Finkle a small compact mirror. He taps it, revealing his long and darkening nails. Brittle and yellow underneath, he opens it. Moving his head, he admires his jawline and hair, messing with it, especially the tiny cowlick in the back.

"I can't wrap my head around a cowlick. I think it should be cut off, but then I might look different. What do you think?"

Finkle walks back up to Tre. He bends down by her face and holds the compact mirror up. Too horrified to speak, she begins to shake as she tries to unravel the rope herself. Finkle stares at her and snaps the compact in her face.

"Half wolf, half human. Now what I want to know is how you ever thought you were normal. I mean," he laughs. "When was the last time you ate? You've been here for months and never ate a thing. Now, why is that?"

He places his hand over hers and whispers in her ear, "Because it's the island that is feeding you." The quick wind of the words makes her give all her attention to him as he walks away. "Allow me to introduce myself. My name is Stanley Jacob Finkle."

From all sides, the dark descendants hiss. Starting slow, deep, and eventually hitting a high-pitch tune like a wrong note as a tuner on a violin turns higher.

"We were lost. But now we have been found."

Tre tries to lean off the wooden seat she's sitting in with everything she has as two Dark Descendants approach. They take the long wooden hand into their hands and lift it, slightly shifting the chair. Finkle begins to hum Frère Jacques, and a deep voice joins him. Tre is still attempting to free herself from the belts.

"No, no."

"But one is lost."

Immediately, Tre is dunked underwater. The bubbles from the chair appear as Finkle smiles.

"So let her be found."

CHAPTER 24
THE BONE DANCE

CATCHY AND TRIUMPHANT, the islanders stand in 1800s outfits. For the men, trousers are flat black, rusty orange, hunter green, and red, like Mother Nature's paintings. There are heels on their buckled shoes, shirts held down by black suspenders, and coats with silver and golden buttons. The women wear fancy dresses with filled-out skirts, wired under the hoop, laced, and tied in the back. Their faces are hidden as they stare through the bones of skinned strangers who have disappeared throughout the years. Leftover flesh hangs from stakes around them.

Islanders standing on the sides, watching as two hands clasp. One hand wears a simple button bracelet, and the other wears a watch that ticks backward as they tighten their grip on each other. The man assists the woman in navigating the brooms in a large spiral. He watches her as she gestures to the islanders; one female reaches out to her, and another, in awe and love, lays her head on her husband's shoulder. As she curtsies, he bows.

A dark and deep waltz breathes an ominous rush through the crowd as the two dances. Some islanders lean in close whispering with silver goblets, while others have love in their eyes as they hold their spouses close.

The two people in the middle begin to twirl: Stanley and Emme. Stanley is dressed in a red and black suit with a loose white shirt, wearing a black bone mask in the shape of a bird skull like a plague doctor. Stanley stops and bends down to kiss the gloved hand, which quickly yanked away. He smiles as he looks up through the eyes of the dead.

"How do you feel?"

The edges of a deep shimmery red dress swirl in the night's air and the candlelight surrounding them. Stopping the bottom of the dress wraps around her slender legs, Emme slowly reveals the dark loose curls of her large ponytail with baby's breath with fall leaves woven inside. Her mask lines her eyes; the bones of a bat with its wings extended.

***

Is it seaweed? A loose rope? Possibly a fisherman's net they lost earlier in the day or even last year. Whatever it is, Tre is becoming tangled within it. She moves back and forth. She tries to break the ropes around her wrist. Tre doesn't care if she breaks her wrist. Twisting and turning, she finally breaks free.

Quickly she moves to her other hand. Around her, the water turns colder as a little slip between her lips. She swallows it. The taste is disgustingly bitter and sharp. She has to forget about it as she continues to work the rope on her other hand.

As she comes to a halt, she notices specks of fabric weaving through the dirt and descending into the bottom of the net. Something shiny is down there. Time is running out. The air left inside her lungs dwindles as little bubbles begin to escape from her nostrils. Her chest tightens as if someone is slowly ringing her lungs like a wet washcloth.

Yanking and pulling on a rope that is not moving, her arm hits something that keeps bumping at her. She turns her head. It's the bloated, gashed body of her deputy and lover on the mainland, Philip. Cement blocks and sandbags are tied to his feet, weighing him down, so he never floats to the surface. A snake weaves through Philip's eye sockets, and another exits his mouth. Bubbles escape her mouth as she screams and flails her arms around.

She jerks her legs, waist, and arms but can't break free. Tre never gives up fighting. Time is fading. The last of her breaths exists.

She drowns. The wooden chair slowly lifts from the water.

"Famished."

Emme floats gracefully toward Stanley, the tips of her small lace-up black boots making designs in the dirt as if tracing a map. He catches her with a long dip, lengthening her torso and arms.

"And you?"

Inside the makeshift coffin, Finkle bangs and screams. He kicks the end of it and breaks the wood, allowing worms, beetles, and scorpions to enter. As he fights to get rid of them, the scorpions sting his legs and arms before making their way to his face. His entire face is covered in small jabs made by the scorpions.

His body contorts like a broken puzzle piece forced into a section where it doesn't belong. His movements slow, and his entire body relaxes as pus and blood ooze from his fresh wounds.

The bugs crawl in and begin to make their homes inside his mouth and ears, as well as inside the wounds they created, widening them. Suddenly, two arms split the wooden coffin's bottom and wraparound Finkle. They pull him deeper into the earth.

"Fresh as a daisy."

On the verge of laughter, Stanley and Emme are distracted by one of the islander's voices.

"To a new life," an Islander shouts out to the crowd.

Stanley rises with Emme from their dip. The islanders cheer with their silver goblets as Stanley and Emme look around at their coven. Over time, the Dark Descendants held hands with the darkness until their new bodies—their ancestors, their doppelgangers—were born at the exact age they died at the hands of the mainlanders. Making sure the traditions were properly passed down and taught until the last two, the brother and sister who started the darkness, are finally born and welcomed back.

Cheering in agreement, the islanders sip their drinks and gulp them all down. For some, modesty is never an issue. While others let the blood trickle down their chins and their mouth edges. Dropping their goblets, they begin to make animal noises and scratch each other like cats on the scratching post with a flirtatious attitude. Most strip their clothes off, mount each other, and indulge in an endless, illicit hunger. Stanley glances around and back at Emme.

"I have something for you."

"Really?"

"Close your eyes."

Excited, Emme places her hands in front of her face. He catches her peeking through the slips of her fingers.

"No peeking."

Rushing to the side of Stanley, a young Islander stands with a small cage. He stands upright and still, never looking at Emme, but smiles and feels honored to even be near her.

"Can I look yet?"

Stanley laughs as he places the tips of his animalistic claws on the cloth. "Open them."

Emme is surprised as Stanley uncovers the box. Inside there are two large rats with wiry hair, long whiskers, and fat. Flipping the lid back, the rats scurry with nowhere to hide.

They scream as he pulls them out by their necks and holds them up beside his face while they flare around. Emme, she puts her hands over her mouth.

"You remember," Emme says, heartfelt.

"A big brother always knows his little sister's favorite snack."

He hands her one. She plays with it for a moment, wriggling and thrashing it around. She soothes it with a click of her tongue. Stanley and Emme intertwine their arms and sink their teeth into the rat's side, ripping the tendons and meat from the skin until their squeaks become silent. The crunch of the rat's bones between her teeth fills Emme with excitement and joy. When he notices a small line of blood streaming out of the corner of her mouth, he smiles under his mask. He rubs the excess blood away with his thumb, and Tre grabs it, sucking and licking it clean while smiling. Her teeth are jagged and filthy. She bites her lower lip as she looks at him. He knows that look.

"Are you still hungry?"

"Yes. But first, can we play a little game?"

"No"

Emme tosses the dead rat to the ground, and her long black tongue swipes the blood and intestines from her lips. She grabs Stanley's collar. Automatically, he throws his hands up in the air. Stanley is not going to argue with her. He wants to make her happy. He shakes his head, causing her to bounce in a place like a little girl.

"There's nothing I wouldn't do for you."

Sabine walks through the foyer with a steel meat cleaver and a closed-top basket, going about her daily routine. Suddenly, Stanley rushes through the front door. Startled, Sabine almost drops the basket as Stanley takes her by the hand. He twirls

Sabine in place. Laughing, Stanley takes the cleaver and basket and places it on the end table. They continue to dance.

"Well, it's about time. I had planned to eat this filling breakfast by myself. But now I don't have to."

"You're never going to eat alone again," Stanley replies and kisses her cheek. Stanley pulls back and reveals Emme. Instantly, Sabine tears up.

"My Emme," Sabine says, lovingly.

"Sabine."

Emme embraces Sabine so tight that she is crushing her spine. "I thought I was never going to see you again. You look exactly like, well..."

Emme pulls back to examine her. From the sides of her eyes, Sabine blinks with her scaly green eyelids. Sabine is the Dark Descendant of the one who found Stanley and Emme when they were dropped in the woods. She will always remember the fire from Stanley and the beauty Emme had. More than anything, she will remember the taste of their father after she ate his brain on his wedding night to their new mother. It was a glorious and unforgettable honeymoon.

"I hope I'm not getting too old, dear. I have missed my darling Emme. "

"Hardly. I think you look better than ever."

"It was a long and stressful job, but it had to be done, taking special care of this guy. Finkle is a rogue—wait. Stanley. My dear, dear boy."

"This is why I call you mother," Stanley grins.

Emme abruptly turns and slaps Stanley on the shoulders, yelling, "Tag, you're it."

Emme bolts up the stairs as quickly as she can. He follows her instinctively but returns and dives his hand into the basket, retrieving a handful of eyeballs before stomping up the stairs. Sabine sighs and shakes her head. "It's good to have them back."

A bloodcurdling scream comes from the kitchen.

"Pipe down in there. I'm coming," Sabine hollers. "I need to get that rack of ribs from the mainlander before he decides to die on me. I enjoy a good morning yell." She makes her way to the kitchen.

———

Stanley moves around the rooms upstairs, looking for Tre. Even in the dark, she has improved. Now that the sun is shining, it should be easier. But it isn't. Tag has evolved into a game of hide and seek.

He cracks the door to Tre's room open, looking around for Emme. He doesn't have to look far because she's in front of her mirror. She is concerned as she stares. He enters and takes a seat beside her. She never takes her gaze away from the drape.

"What if it's not real? I mean. What if this is only temporary?"

He puts his arm over her shoulder, and says, "It's not. We have waited so long…"

"Exactly, we have waited for so long. Every time we return, the bodies fail. We fail." Emme shouts, hitting her chest hard and loudly like a hollow tree.

"It's not going to happen this time. We are in the bodies we deserve. Our people made sure of it. I made sure of it. They sacrificed, I sacrificed for us. You."

———

The doppelgangers stand strong behind the brother with their arms raised and palms turned up. The priest and the townsmen rush toward them. Each one is struck down; never fighting for their lives, they give up and fall into the anger of the mainlanders. While some have their bodies bashed in with sledgehammers, others have their throats sliced, and other heads are decapitated and set on spikes.

When the coven is dead, the priest and townsmen rejoice, forgetting the words the brother whispered before he was ripped limb from limb.

"We shall return. Your descendants will pay by our hands."

Stanley grabs the drape and prepares to remove it. Emme stops him.

"What if they are there trying to get out?"

"Then we make the most of what time we have together."

"They are going to haunt us just like the others. I don't want to go back to the dark."

Stanley cradles her face. "Then I'll figure out how to permanently get rid of them. Or hold them off until the next."

"Neither had children, Stanley. We are the last."

"Trust me."

Spreading the wrinkles on her dress, Emme shakes her head once as she touches her stomach, anxious. She shuts her eyes. A tear falls down her cheek as she feels the wind pull away from the drape. Stanley drops it as he glances into the mirror.

Emme's breathing is rapid, so Stanley takes her hand in his and comforts her. She folds her body into his and refuses to look. He turns her around again. She opens her eyes. She holds back her sobs. Her appearance is not worn or soiled; there is no blood on her dress, and there is no gaping hole in the middle of her chest from profuse bleeding. Her skin isn't rotting or falling off. She's not as repulsive as the dead bodies in their above-ground cemetery basement or the ones Sabine is cutting and freezing.

Emme is young, vibrant, and, above all, in her descendant's body. Her body. As far as the mainlanders are concerned, the ugliness that normally follows the reflections of the dark descendants no longer exists, instead of the luscious locks of waves and bouncy curls. Emme's skin isn't rubbery and saggy but smooth and subtle. Her eyes are bright and sparkling in the sunlight.

Emme touches her face, and Stanley steps behind her.

"I told you. We are last."

"We are perfect for once. Better than we used to be."

Emme takes a step forward, smiling at herself and then at Stanley. He gently presses his hand against her shoulder. She takes it in her hands, feels his skin inside, and hears the blood vessels bumping into the walls of his flesh. She turns back to the mirror. It's the first time in centuries Emme has seen herself. Half of her is stunning, and her inner light shines brighter than Tre's ever could. But the other half. Stanley is a half-black wolf and half-human in the mirror, while Emme is a half-human and half-white panther. Stanley is in awe as he looks her up and down.

"You are going to look beautiful as we split the water and walk onto the mainland. What will you do first, sister?"

"Devour every fucking one of them."

With a sinister smile, Stanley says, "Welcome back to the living, dear sister."

They laugh uncontrollably as darkness swallows their human reflections in the mirror, allowing only a sliver of light to shine on their hideous sides.

To my husband and daughter, thank you for understanding that when I am in my writing hole, typing away on weekends and late into the night, and when I ramble through a scene or chapter, whether you know what is happening, y'all always agree. I appreciate it. I love y'all more every day.

Mom and Dad, I will continue to thank you for introducing me to horror. It was the best thing ever, as we can see. Without y'all, I know I would not be here. You made sure I had opportunities that helped cultivate the writer in me. I love you so much. Plus, y'all are the best critics I could ever ask for. And when I say, to be honest, you are, In the best way, which makes me work and write harder.

To Monique Asher (*Don't Eat the Pie and The Red Knot*) *and* Alyssa Alessi (*Izzy Hoffman is Not a Witch*) for always being there. Thank you for never holding back when I send some crazy things. I respect and appreciate it. I am so glad we are champions for each other. There are many writers in this world, and you two are phenomenal writers who scare me with their words. I admire and respect you both.

To my readers, I especially want to thank you for taking any time out of your day to read my stories. My characters thank you as well. I want you to know I have been writing for many years, but I never had the guts to do it for a long time. But it is y'all who makes me want to continue, plus I want to scare your socks off. I have many plans. Scary, creepy plans—as I like to say, have a horror of a day.

ABOUT THE AUTHOR

Stacey L. Pierson is a horror writer living in Louisiana with her husband and daughter. She has been drawn to horror since she can remember. She is the author of the poem, My Little Dragonfly Collected Whispers, The International Library of Poetry, in 2008. Her first novel, Vale, a young adult bayou murder mystery in 2022, the haunting poem, Carnival in Abditory Literary Journal Issue One: Mirabilia in 2022, were published two days apart.